Debi Evans J

The Secret Society

Of

Dragon Protectors

'The Silver Claw'

For Archie

Debi Evans

Published by Debi Evans & John MacPherson

Cover design / illustration and chapter illustrations by John MacPherson

Published by Debi Evans & John MacPherson
Printed by the MPG Books Group Bodmin and King's Lynn

Copyright © Debi Evans & John MacPherson 2010
Cover design & all illustrations Copyright © John MacPherson 2010

ISBN   978-0-9554661-4-4

Books by
Debi Evans & John MacPherson
In

THE SECRET SOCIETY

OF

DRAGON PROTECTORS

Series

'The Dragon's Tale'
'The Cor Stan'
'A Shadow in Time'
'The City Guardians'

Contents

'For my dear Dad, John James, who wants to know what happens next....and for Audrey Evans because she encourages me' D.E.

'While writing this story you were never far from my thoughts Steve. Hong Kong will never be the same without Sidders and you are dearly missed by all. For Steven J Sidley.' J.M.

Chapter 1

'Dragons From Beyond'

The house was still and silent with the gentle vibration of a boiler in the kitchen the only sound of activity. Upstairs, in a bedroom, an alarm clock shone brightly on the table as the green digital numbers seared '**2:47am**' into the darkness. A warm feather duvet was tucked tightly under the chin of a teenage boy as he lay on his back. In the darkness concerned expressions fluttered across his face as his eye's moved frantically behind tightly closed eyelids. He began to murmur incoherently through tightened lips as his head moved from side to side; a nightmare disturbing the stillness of sleep.

Inside that dream Angus had just replayed his battle with Felspar for the umpteenth time, but unlike the event that took place last year and the reality he now knew to be true, the lad witnessed the black dragon drag his wounded body to a nearby stream where he scraped off some of the precious stones from his stomach. To the lad's horror, he witnessed Felspar staunch the wound before staggering into a nearby forest to hide in the dark undergrowth. Helpless and unable to call out, he watched as both he and Pyrra arrived at the spot where the discarded jewels lay on the riverbed. It confused him to think that he was looking at something that had never happened and he could not understand why this particular twist kept forcing itself on his memories, but unlike the usual fuzzy mixed up image a nightmare would normally take, this one was very sharp indeed. Just as that thought hit his mind the images fluttered and faded to be replaced by the dark blue dragon that had disturbed his dreams last year.

The dragon appeared to be intertwined with events that had turned out to be true. It had helped Angus come to some conclusions on what Felspar had been trying to achieve; however since then he had not been revisited by the merest of images and Angus had put it all down to his imagination and déjà-vu. Tonight was different.

The familiar looking dragon before him appeared so real, Angus felt he could reach out and touch him. The shape of the horns and snout were unmistakably male, but it was the eyes that drew the young protector's attention. They were green, but not just any green; these were the same green as Pyrra's and if he focused on only the eyes he was looking at his best friend and comrade.

"You must follow me, Angus!" said the stranger.

'Did I just hear that?' thought the lad to himself, the dragon's voice was so clear.

"Yes, you did!" the dragon surprisingly replied. "And this is the strongest link I've managed to forge with you yet. I need to show you something and you must follow me!"

"But who are you? And where are you?" Angus called out anxiously, believing the dragon was speaking to him using the same technique the late Ward Barfoot had used prior to the Trials of the Cor Stan.

"I will explain all that later when you are ready to understand, but for now you must trust me..." the dragon's green eyes seemed to pierce Angus' subconscious. "Can you do that?"

The dragon was a stranger to him, but Angus stared into the somehow familiar eyes for a second or two.

"Yes... I can" replied the protector at last.

"Excellent!" smiled the dragon. "Now, in order for you to go where I go, you will need to jump on my back" he added as he turned around.

Angus did not understand what was going on, and although he was dubious about what was in store he decided, since it was all a dream anyway, he could not come to any harm.

No sooner had he simulated jumping on the dragon's back than the whole image began to blur around them. It struck Angus that the dragon had appeared to him in his bedroom and that he had not seen this as unusual. Now the only thing he could properly focus on was the back of the blue dragon's head and he was surprised at the messages his senses sent him. As colours and images blurred and flew past them, Angus rubbed his hands over the scales of the dragon; shockingly he could feel them! He knew, and kept telling himself over and over, that none of what was happening was genuine; and yet his senses told him that the dragon he now sat on was as solid as rock and very real indeed.

"We're here!" said the dragon, suddenly jolting Angus from reverie.

"Where's here exactly?" asked the lad.

"The here is not important right now…" replied the dragon, "but it is important that you see what is about to happen and know that it is in your future!"
Without another word the dragon motioned for Angus to get down and as he did so the images around them began to coalesce into more recognisable objects.

As Angus watched he could see the floor became clearer and they stood on a floor made up of finely cut stones. He watched as the stones continued to materialise until the walls appeared and, as if by infection, other areas started to materialise. As Angus sat open mouthed, a whole room developed around him and to his great surprise he could see Pyrra standing quite near him. Instinctively he wanted to call out to her but he knew it was not really her and just part of this crazy dream!

"This part you will need to do on your own as I need to focus my powers on maintaining this illusion, but I will not be far from you now and I will return soon!"

Angus turned to look for the strange blue dragon but he was gone. He wished he knew what was going to happen next and what 'soon' meant, but that was immediately forgotten when he heard sardonic laughter behind him; it was a voice he knew very well.

Turning around slowly Angus was now in a room full of people and dragons, however none of them were fully in focus and he struggled to recognise anyone other than Pyrra. What was more bizarre was he appeared to be the centre of attention. At least as far as he could tell! Desperately confused he tried to grasp the basics of his surroundings. He was in an extremely large but simply decorated room which appeared to be quite symmetrical in design. In it stood several men, none of whom he knew, but they did appear to be guards of some sort. Apart from Pyrra he could see other dragons, and at first he thought one of them was the strange dream dragon, but he couldn't be sure. Turning to his left he saw other figures that, judging from their attire, could have been Georgina and Kadin. They stood beside another lad he could not make out at all and then his eyes fixed on an old man as his face came into focus. More perplexing still, the old man appeared to see Angus, and as the young protector watched, he winked and smiled as if he knew Angus was there. This bizarre incident was immediately driven from the lad's mind as his eyes met with the person responsible for the malevolent laughter.

"Tell me Angus, how did you manage to escape my guards?" asked Meredith Quinton-Jones.

Dumbfounded by the sight of Meredith, Angus could not answer, and besides, he did not know where he had escaped from!

"No witty remarks? Perhaps he needs a little persuasion!" growled a voice from behind.

Angus spun round to be met with the fearsome sight of Felspar not more than two metres away from him!

Things were becoming too much for the young lad now and he was struggling to take it all in.

"Now, now Felspar; you leave him be" purred Meredith, "I have a much better method of dealing with this little thorn!"

Felspar sneered as he walked past Angus to join Meredith; the young protector's gaze never faltering as he watched the black dragon swagger to Meredith's side.

"Pyrra, I command you to kill Angus Munro!" shouted Meredith maniacally.

Slowly Angus turned to Pyrra, his head swimming as nothing made any sense in this madness. As he looked up into Pyrra's green eyes he could see the conflict within her. The green dragon's body vibrated as she fought to resist the command. 'Surely she was still his best friend and would never hurt him!' he thought.

"Attack him now, Pyrra!" screamed Meredith. "I order you to kill him!"

Angus watched as Pyrra's eyes glazed over with a faraway look. Now he was looking at a stranger and her body stopped vibrating. She reared in front of him and, with her right claw raised high, prepared to attack him! 'No!' yelled Angus in his head, 'how can this be happening?'

"Pyrra it's me, Angus, remember?" he shouted. "Pyrra, please, it's me!"

He started to shake and from somewhere someone called his name. The young protector looked around frantically for the person calling his name, Meredith's laughter getting louder and louder. The person calling might be able to help, but no-one was there and the maniacal laughter was so loud now he could hardly think. He looked up at Pyrra again just as her claw slashed downwards towards him!

Chapter 2

'Another Gathering'

"Wake up, Son!" said the voice, as Angus felt his whole body being shaken.

Angus opened his eyes to find his mum sitting beside him on his bed. She looked really upset and concerned and had him upright with her hands on his shoulders. To make sure he was awake, she shook him again.

"Wake up Angus, you're having a bad dream!" she said.

"Mum... I'm awake... I'm okay!" he replied groggily.

"You were shouting in your sleep and woke us up" she said with concern, not releasing her grip.

Angus looked around his room and could see his dad standing in the doorway.

"You okay, Son?" he asked, "You gave your mother quite a turn there and I think you've woken up the whole street!" he added rubbing his head.

Angus pondered what had just transpired in his dream and was thinking that things were not okay. How he wished he could tell his parents about his secret life as a dragon protector and about all the adventures he and Pyrra had whilst searching for hidden dragons, or tell them that a mad woman had tried to kill him only a few weeks ago!

"I'm fine Dad" he replied instead, "Just a nightmare."

"Probably all that pizza you ate for dinner last night!" added his dad before turning to go back to bed. "I'm off back to sleep as I've got those deliveries to make in a couple of hours. Night love, see you in a minute!" he said to his wife as he left.

Angus looked at the digital clock, the numbers brightly flashing on and off as if waiting to be set.

"You must have hit the buttons when you were thrashing about; I thought you were having a fit when I came in" said his mum in explanation, having followed his gaze. "By the way, who is Pyrra?" she asked.

Angus froze, hardly daring to look at his mum, and immediately worried about what she might have heard him say in his sleep.

"Oh... just some character from a horror movie I watched recently... I think!" he mumbled.

"Well *I think* you should give horror movies a rest for a while" she replied, and flicking the hair from his forehead affectionately, added, "Now back to sleep for a few hours and no more nightmares!"

Angus lay down and smiled at his mum as she tucked him in and went to the door. He had not been treated like this in a long time and amongst his embarrassment he felt comforted by the fact that his parents cared so much for him, even if they rarely showed it.

"Do you want the light left on, Son?" she asked with her hand hovering over the switch.

"No Mum, I'm fine" he smiled.

The door shut behind her and with the room now in darkness again, Angus set about trying to unscramble the dream.

"No way I'm going to go back to sleep now" he said to himself, and he lay staring into space as the images and thoughts reeled through his mind once more.

Two hours later Angus heard his dad get up for work and even though it was Saturday he decided he might as well get up early too. He quickly washed and brushed his teeth before heading downstairs where he found his dad already tucking into his cereal with the morning paper propped up in front of his face.

"Hello Son!" said his dad. "I didn't expect to see you up and around so early after this morning's little drama!" he smiled.

"Couldn't sleep" replied Angus stifling a yawn.

"Nightmare still bothering you then?" asked his father.

"No... I just couldn't sleep" replied Angus as he found a bowl and began to pour some cereal.

His dad just smiled and went back to reading the article he was on and after scanning what he thought was the relevant pieces of interest on that page, turned the paper around to view the next page. Angus watched his dad and smiled as he realised how habitual his father was. He always folded the paper over on itself to make it more rigid. That way he could read it upright and not take up the whole table with it; something his mum hated. As he was about to look away his eye caught part of a picture on the page facing him which was partially obscured by his dad's hand. Angus leant forward and peered at the picture to try and see it better.

"Do you want to read this after me Son?" asked Donald dropping the paper to one side.

"No it's okay Dad, I just thought I recognised someone, that's all" replied Angus taking a spoonful of cereal that had been floating halfway between the bowl and his mouth as if it was on a bungee rope.

"Which one?" asked his dad turning the paper again.

Angus pointed to the picture he had spotted and sure enough there was Meredith Quinton-Jones pictured leaving an old building.

"Oh she's a real crack pot; that one!" laughed his dad. "She only tried to rob the Natural History Museum a few weeks back! Claimed she was retrieving dragon eggs but they found only replica dinosaur eggs on her and now they've let her off due to medical reasons..."

"THEY'VE WHAT?" shouted Angus, spluttering honey coated puffs all over his dad.

Angus' father was shocked at his son's reaction and then suddenly burst out laughing. Angus flushed with embarrassment at his outburst.

"Sorry Dad" he said as he tried to pick up the puffs.

"That's okay Son but between bad dreams and now this, you're having a brilliant start to the day... are you sure you don't want to stay in bed? It might be safer for the rest of us!" he chuckled.

Angus saw the funny side of his actions and began to snigger with his dad as he mimicked Angus' outburst. Soon they were laughing so hard that they were fit to burst and only subsided when the lad's mum came into the kitchen.

"So much for my long lie-in then!" she said as she entered, fastening her dressing gown.

"Sorry love" replied Donald; "We were just having a laugh at this poor lady".

"Oh her... what a shame; must be the stress of running her own company that did it."

Angus could not help but smile at his mum; trust her show compassion and take pity on someone regardless of what they had done.

Once his dad had finished with the newspaper, Angus read the article in full and found out that Meredith had indeed been released due to medical grounds. Apparently her expensive lawyers had earned their large fees by convincing the judge that she was stressed due to work pressures and had 'simply experienced an unfortunate episode'. This was backed up by several important people, including the scientist Angus had seen at her offices. They claimed to have all played along for fear Meredith would damage herself and that they never expected her to take things as far as she had. She was to remain in the country under strict medical care at her country estate. Angus put the paper down and looked at the ceiling in dismay. Perhaps that was what the dream was about, just some sort of strange nightmare from his subconscious to let him know she was to be released. He had been quite happy these last few weeks knowing that she was going to jail and now that she had apparently avoided that certainty he was not too sure what the future held for Georgina and himself. At the thought of Georgina he smiled realising he would be meeting her at The Gathering today, and he began to gobble up the rest of his cereal.

An hour later, Angus walked to the end of his street and waited in the cold winter sunlight for his best and most trusted friend. It was not difficult for him to say this as he had been through so many adventures with her that he could never see a time when he would trust anyone as much as he trusted Pyrra. She had saved his life at least twice and he had also saved hers, but it was not just that. He took a sweet from his pocket, but did not eat it. There was an unbreakable bond forged between them so strong that they could almost hear each other's thoughts. He heard a soft flutter behind him and feeling the rush of wind knew that she had landed. He turned and held out the cough candy he had taken from his jacket pocket.

"So you did see me then?" asked the green dragon smiling broadly. "For a second there I thought I was going to catch you out!"

"Not likely!" laughed the lad.

As she savoured the candy from his hand Angus looked into her green eyes and his mind flashed back to the point in his dream where her eyes had glazed over unrecognisably. As she looked at him now he could never imagine her ever hurting him intentionally.

"You look troubled... penny for your thoughts?" she asked, concerned at his expression.

"Oh... er... nothing... just something I read about this morning that upset me" he replied not wanting to reveal the contents of his dream to her.

At her prompting he began to tell her about the news article and that Meredith was now free again. By the time he had finished they were in mid air and on their way to meet Georgina and the others in the village of Marnham.

They landed in the old cemetery at the side of the church and since Angus could not see the others yet he left Pyrra to locate the dragons as he went off to find Georgina. It was not before long that he returned avidly discussing with Georgina the failings of the justice system when he noticed Pyrra had found Georgina's dragon companion, Wymarc. The green dragon seemed to have grown very fond of the dark blue dragon and it occurred to Angus that she had found a new dragon companion to replace Godroi since he had taken up residence permanently guarding the Cor Stan in Krubera with Finian Tek. Pyrra had been visiting Marnham more and more these days and Angus decided to tease her about this later.

"Good morning all! Shall we get going then?" called Hugh Penfold as he bounced along the path behind them; tripping over his long scarf as usual and blowing into his hands to alleviate the cold.

"Yes Daddy... but let me fix this before you injure yourself again!" Georgina added, making a fuss over him and adjusting his clothing.

It was not long before they were up in the air again and from the privileged vantage point he had from Pyrra's back Angus took in the now familiar views along the journey to Krubera. They had just past over London as he recalled the night he and Pyrra had been chased by Meredith and her henchmen. She had helicopters flying at them and had tried to kill Pyrra and the City Guardians, the group of dragons sworn to protect the British capital. He hoped that they would all make it to the latest Gathering, which was the first to be held since Angus and Georgina had returned from London some weeks back. He realised that he had been leaning forward along Pyrra's neck and her warmth shielded him from the cold elements. It was not long before he fell asleep; images of the previous night flitting in and out of his mind with Meredith's mocking laughter the most prominent sound in his thoughts.

Chapter 3

'Justice Undone'

Meredith Quinton-Jones considered her reflection in the mirror. She was not happy with the cut of the vermillion suit she was wearing and it vexed her immensely that the tailor had not managed to catch the shape exactly as she had instructed. She was used to getting what she wanted and Meredith had no time for people who failed her and she made a mental note to have several words with the over-priced dressmaker. The words would not be pleasant, but they would be terminal. It was tiresome as she would have to find someone better; but for now it would have to do. She was meeting her court appointed 'therapist' any minute and she wanted to portray the correct image if she were to remain out of jail. She made her way downstairs and into the drawing room where she usually met her guests. There was a chaise lounge which would suffice as a couch should she need to dramatise things that far. As she passed a portrait of her father on the stairs she thought about how pointless it was for the court to have this person assess her when her own therapists had already given them all the paperwork they required. Reaching the bottom of the stairs she turned and walked towards the drawing room and decided to get it over and done with. Setting her demeanour before she opened the door, her face portrayed a mixture of confusion and innocence; a bit like that of a lost child. Meredith deserved an Oscar.

The man in the room turned to the door as he heard it open. He had been dreading this encounter for some time as he had heard stories about how demanding and difficult this woman could be. He had read a lot about her in his lead up to this session and by all accounts she had been a ruthless and robust business woman; equally at home on an oil rig as she was behind a desk.

"Good morning Ms Quinton-Jones, I'm very pleased to meet you" he managed to say without stammering.

"Hello... Doctor Rust" replied Meredith with hesitation. Meredith stood in front of the doctor looking uncertainly around the room. For his part the doctor could not believe he had met the right woman. 'Surely this was not the woman he had read about?' he thought. It clearly was her, but he could see she was not herself and proffered a seat for her to sit on.

"Please sit here Ms Quinton-Jones" he said.
She smiled wanly at him and sat on the edge of the seat looking uncomfortable.

"Please call me Meredith" she said to him, but all the time she looked around the room and never at him directly. It appeared to the doctor that this lady was clearly traumatised in some way and he wanted to help her but he was only here to assess her and he was sure that her own doctors were more than capable of helping her.

"How do you feel, Ms; sorry, Meredith?"
The woman in front of him looked furtively around the room before she finally answered.

"I'm fine" she whispered, "Just a little on edge."

"Why so?" he enquired further.
Again Meredith did not answer right away, but this time she leant forward and looked under the table by the window.

"I don't want anyone to hear me" she whispered again. Dr. Rust made some notes in his diary and continued his questioning; this was something he had to delve into for his report.

"Whom exactly do you think will hear you, Meredith?" he asked softly.
This time she checked behind him and then smiling with satisfaction she sat back down and answered.

"It's okay... they're not here" she replied in a normal tone.

Dr. Rust made another note in his diary; this was going to take longer than he thought and he started to probe further.

Almost an hour later Dr. Rust left the large mansion that was the ancestral home of the Quinton-Jones family. He turned towards the butler.

"Millar, promise me you will look after Ms Quinton-Jones" he said earnestly.

"One will do one's best sir!" replied the butler, his serious expression never faltering.

"Right... well... that's good then... thank you" replied Dr. Rust, relieved that he had done his job.

He turned and walked across the gravel driveway to his car, the butler watching him from the door until he had started to move off. Millar closed the large front door and returned to the Drawing Room where his mistress was waiting. She stood at the window watching the retreating car, making its way down the drive to the main gate.

"The gentleman requested that I look after you madam; I trust that will not be required?" he enquired matter-of-factly.

"Good god no!" she replied, "I'm fine Millar and you jolly well know it!"

"Quite. Madam obviously made a very strong impression on the young man"

"He's a fool like the rest of them Millar and I take no pleasure from duping a fool!"

"Would you like me to pack your travelling trunk madam?"

"Yes Millar" she replied absently, "and ask Felspar to meet me in the study."

"He is already there madam" answered the butler. At that he turned and left to attend to his household duties.

Meredith entered the Study and found the black dragon lying on the rug in front of the fire. This might have fooled some people into thinking he was a pet dog; ready to answer the master's call, but this was Felspar and he was no pet!

"Ah you're finally finished!" he said lazily from the floor without moving or opening his eyes.

"Yes... it was tedious and boring but necessary to convince that pompous judge that I am *not in my normal frame of mind and in need of specialist care and attention*!" she replied in a mocking voice as if reciting something she had learned by heart.

"Well you would go and get yourself caught!" taunted the dragon as he took up most of the floor with his size.

"That's enough from you, thank you!" she snapped. "I will be ready to leave tomorrow, but tell me about this place again?"

The black dragon sighed and reluctantly shifted his position to address the woman he now thought of as the only tolerable human he knew. He sat up and absently rubbed at a scar on his chest which itched from time to time. It

irritated him but not as much as the thought of how he had received it. His hatred for Angus Munro was raw and the thought of the young protector fuelled the dragon's bitterness.

"The place is remote and we will not be discovered, but retrieving this object will not be easy. We will need someone to navigate a way through and it should be someone expendable!" explained the dragon.

Meredith paced the room deep in thought, Felspar watched her intently as this usually meant she had a plan cooking in her head and he hoped it would mean some action as he was bored with sitting around and it had already been a couple of days since he returned from China. Finally she stopped pacing.

"You say we need someone expendable?" she said, drumming her nails on the desk.

"I'm sure you can find one of your minions to do the job but it needs to be a small one" added Felspar even though he knew she was not really asking his opinion.

"Oh I would not use one of them" she grinned, "I think I can come up with someone better than a mere minion!"

Chapter 4

'The Joining'

Anyone who is interested in dragons will already know that they are attracted to bright shiny objects. In particular, jewels; which they collect whenever and wherever possible. If you are lucky enough to find a dragon, you will almost certainly find treasure; however what is less well known is that when baby dragons are born their mothers show them how to roll on the floor so that jewels stick to their undersides. This gives the dragons protection for their weaker scales and acts like armour. Angus found out that since it is difficult to find jewels lying around, the dragons have begun to store them in a safe place; Krubera, where the birthing caves are located. They will also retain any jewels discarded after the death of a dragon, and when the young fire whelps have enough strength in their wings for the flight to Krubera, they are taken to the Birthing Caves and shown this very important skill. He liked to think of it as the dragons' way of recycling, but he knew the most important jewel for every dragon was the Heart Stone, and it was for this reason that everyone was gathering at Krubera today; to witness Aedan and Ceamantya receiving their precious and power giving Dragonore.

Angus awoke just as Pyrra had started her descent towards Krubera, the home of the Cor Stan, hidden in the hostile mountains of Georgia in Eastern Europe. Already he could see a number of dragons and protectors making their way down into the deep cave system. He marvelled at the sight before him and felt proud that he and Pyrra had played a part in finding many of the dragons that would be gathered today. In fact by the time they landed it was obvious it was not going to be an easy task to reach the inner sanctum of Krubera and Angus and Pyrra's eventual arrival inside the Birthing Caves was somewhat later than planned. Their progress from the entrance cave was further hampered when they were mobbed by a variety of dragons and protectors. Word of the pairs exploits and achievements in London had spread amongst the dragon protecting community. Everyone wanted to exchange a few words of congratulation for saving the precious dragon eggs from Meredith.

Twenty minutes after landing on the mountain the duo had only just made it through the shimmering wall that hid the entrance to the dragon's secret cave system.

"Wonderful work in London Angus!" enthused Halla.

"We heard all about your adventure from Rathlin and you are both very brave!" added Lars as he patted both Georgina and Angus heavily on the shoulder.

The congratulations went on and on and when Angus eventually got to the Mirror Cave he had lost Georgina in the throng of protectors and dragons.

After what seemed like ages, Angus finally reached the Cor Stan and he took a moment to study the great rock. Every time he saw the Heart Stone he was sure he could sense power from it; like it was a living organism. He knew it was not alive, but he sensed more energy from it every time he visited Krubera and he could not help but think that the Cor Stan had something to do with the strange things that were happening to him recently. Shaking himself loose from his thoughts, Angus spotted Georgina and started to move towards her, but again he was grabbed by another well wisher who was talking to a familiar dragon.

"Angus!" bellowed Liam, "We were just talking about you, mate!"

The young Irish lad was the same age as Angus and his red spiky hair made him stand out against the mottled green and brown of Wulfric; one of the City Guardians.

"Hi Liam, Wulfric; how are you both?" asked Angus politely.

"I am fine, thank you Angus and it appears that you are very well thought of in the SSDP" replied Wulfric in his usual serious tone.

"Well I don't know about that..." said Angus blushing.

"Here he goes being all humble again. If it was me I'd be strutting around like this!" joked Liam as he started to walk around with his chest inflated.

Surprisingly, the normally stolid Wulfric burst into laughter and everyone in the vicinity stopped what they were doing to stare at him. Infected by the laughter of the dragon both Liam and Angus joined him and it took them some time to stop as the red haired lad continued his comedic antics. Eventually Angus managed to peel himself away from them and spotting Georgina again he moved swiftly to her side, giving her arm a squeeze just as the Leader of the Secret Society of Dragon Protectors called The Gathering to order.

Rathlin Tek hushed the assembled crowd by holding up his arm. Every dragon and protector in the great cavern turned to face him in expectant silence. Angus looked for Ward Godroi but the golden dragon was nowhere to be seen. After the adventures in London, Rathlin had commented on the unusual powers that had been displayed by Angus. He had told the young protector that both he and Godroi would need to discuss this with him and, as yet, that conversation had not taken place. He wondered if they would discuss it today as Rathlin began to speak to the assembly.

"It is my extreme pleasure to welcome so many of you here today" he intoned. "Indeed it does me proud to see that our numbers have once again increased with the addition of the City Guardians!"

This announcement was met with growling bellows from the dragons and cheers from the protectors. Angus could see that not all of the City Guardians were present and he guessed that some of them were still in London carrying out their duty; which was to watch over the great Capital and keep its inhabitants from harm.

As the excitement died down again Rathlin took on a more serious tone.

"It is with great regret that I tell you it was once again one of our own protectors that tried to undermine the very core value on which our society is based."

The cavern became so silent that Angus could hear the drips of water falling from the stalactites' into the mirror pool.

"If it were not for the single minded determination of Angus Munro, we would not be here today to celebrate this momentous occasion."

As the assembled crowd shouted their agreement with Rathlin, Georgina nudged Angus in the ribs whilst whispering in his ear.

"And getting us into heaps of trouble while he's at it!" she giggled.

Angus turned to end up with his face almost touching hers and immediately turned bright red with the usual embarrassment he met all these situations with. He turned to face Rathlin again in an attempt to hide this whilst Rathlin continued to sum up the feelings of the assembled group quite succinctly by thanking Georgina and the City Guardians for the part they played in the retrieval of the dragon eggs. Angus vaguely listened to the rest of the speech as he was too preoccupied with the memory of Georgina's voice in his ear.

"Indeed there would not be a 'Joining' ceremony taking place in Krubera this day if it were not for the group you see before you and they epitomise what this society stands for!" concluded Rathlin with his arms outstretched towards The City Guardians, Georgina and Angus.

The cavern erupted in cheering and applause which appeared to shake the very walls of the underground cave system. As the noise subsided Rathlin again calling for order and reminded everyone of the solemnity of the occasion. They were here today to witness something that had not been seen in at least 1000 years. No dragon had received their Heart Stone in this way since before the Great Hibernation and it was an historic moment indeed.

The sombre silence was interrupted by a great kafuffle in an archway to the left of the assembly and everyone turned to look round. Two baby dragons noisily romped through the gap and stopped short in front of the Gathering. It had been a long flight from Calmor, but the fire whelps were as full of mischief and bounding energy as two playful puppies. Their mother, Rhys, tried to admonish them but, as always, she was serene and graceful in her manner. She could not suppress a proud motherly smile as her two lively offspring bounded into the great cavern making an entrance. The twins stopped dead in their tracks when faced with so many watchful eyes. After a few seconds they noticed Angus and all insecurities pushed to one side as the two fire whelps bounded forwards to administer their usual greeting to him. The crowd erupted in laughter as Angus was subjected to a slobbery dragon wash which covered his entire face.

Rhys herself had been hailed as *Maest Modor* by Godroi. At times she did not feel like a 'Great Mother' at all as the pair proved a bit of a handful. She had already had words with Godroi about that and as he walked silently, but none the less majestically into the cavern behind them she recalled he had promised to find someone to help instruct them in the ancient dragon lore as both she and their father Sterling were too young to have this knowledge. She was keen to see whom he had come up with for this task, but was once again called into action as the twins had decided that Angus was clean enough and had started to playfully wrestle each other again.

Angus watched the two youngsters as he wiped dragon drool from his face with his sleeve. Ceamantya was slightly smaller than her brother, but definitely the bossier and smarter of the two. Using her superior cunning she wrestled Aedan to the ground, tumbling and nipping until, suddenly aware again of the many eyes staring at her, she paused for a moment. They had come to a halt, mid tumble, at the feet of Godroi and the focus of attention shifted to the Ward as the magnificent golden dragon stood in front of the Cor Stan. He raised his claw ready to

address the
Gathering and
Angus could feel
Pyrra tense as his
gaze met hers. He
was her oldest
dragon friend and
the two were still
very close despite
his elevation to

Ward and the geographical distance placed between them.

For the first time humans would witness a dragon obtain its very first precious stone! This was the moment when the dragon joined with the Cor Stan as it embedded Dragonore into the soft underside of a dragon's skin. At a signal from Ward Godroi, the dragons sat back on their haunches. Now the moment had come, and not a sound could be heard in the cave as Godroi took up a piece of Dragonore from the base of the Cor Stan and carefully placed it on first Ceamantya's chest, and then Aedan's. He had placed it right over their heart and at once the Dragonore began to glow as all the others in the cavern did as well. Angus felt sure the whelps were receiving their dragon powers through the ancient stone and indeed he felt his own Dragonore pulse additional heat into his chest where he kept it in a small pouch hung around his neck.

"Welcome my young friends. You are now a part of the Cor Stan and connected to the life blood that flows through all of us!" said Godroi to the young dragons.

Finian stepped forward and without a word opened a box that Angus recognised. It was the box used by Rathlin to collect the jewels left behind when both Hereward and Barfoot had passed away. He had often wondered where it had gone and now he watched Finian open the box towards Godroi.

"As is our tradition we will reuse that which was left behind" said Godroi as he scooped some of the jewels from the box with his claw and scattered them onto the cave floor.

Both fire whelps had been taught by their mother Rhys how to gather the stone and they both got down on their bellies in the manner they had been shown. Each had selected suitable stones on the floor of the cave and rolled on them so that they stuck to their young dragon skin. Angus knew as the dragons grew, their skin would harden around the jewels, keeping them firmly in place. The fire whelps stood up to display their newly acquired jewels.

"The joining is complete and now is the time for celebration!" announced Godroi to rapturous applause.

After the appreciation had died down, Angus and Georgina approached the twins and Faris, leader of the City guardians also reacquainted himself with the young dragons.

"Well Angus it is good to see you again my friend" said the large black dragon.

Angus recalled their first encounter which had not gone quite so well. Faris had aggressively rejected their offer of help and support from the SSDP and had forbidden them to interfere in the business of the City Guardians. However, upon hearing that Angus had crossed swords with Felspar, the twin brother of Faris; the leader had mellowed his stance and had since become a great friend and ally to Angus.

"You look tired. Are you not sleeping well?" asked the black dragon.

"Now that you mention it Faris, he does look jaded. What have you been up to Angus?" asked Georgina with concern.

"I'm fine... just not getting too much sleep recently!" replied Angus dismissively.

"What's this about a lack of sleep?" asked Rathlin as he joined the group.

"Angus was just telling us why he looks so tired" answered Georgina staring at him intently.

"Not having strange dreams again are we Angus?" joked Rathlin.

Angus murmured a barely audible 'no' and tried to change the subject by commenting on the article he had read about Meredith.

"Did you see that they have decided to allow Meredith to go free?" Angus said quickly.

Rathlin studied the young man for a moment and Angus felt that the leader of the SSDP was about to pursue the reason behind his tiredness, but instead he smiled.

"Yes I did and it was very disheartening to say the least" he replied.

"Do you think we should place a body guard with these two?" Angus asked pointing to the young dragons as they wrestled around on the floor again.

"I have already done so" replied Rathlin.

"Really... who is it?" asked Georgina expecting him to point to Faris.

"That would be telling and I rather think I will let Godroi announce it later. For now, we will get these two ready to meet him" he replied mysteriously before walking towards the gambolling fire whelps.

The gathering broke off into groups of dragons and humans all discussing the society and how the Awakening was progressing. Angus could not help notice that Georgina was very pleased about something and he was also aware the she was anxious to share her news.

"Have you heard of the schools competition to write a guide for teenagers to Kew Gardens?" She asked, eventually giving in and deciding not to wait for Angus to enquire.

"Yeah I did see something about that, but it's not really my thing" he replied.
It was no secret that Angus was keener on drawing than writing; especially when it involved dragons.

"I bet you entered though" he teased Georgina, gently.

"Better than that; I've WON!" she smirked triumphantly redefining the underlying current of rivalry between the two, despite their close friendship. "I will be spending the day at Kew next Saturday with my pen poised. Perhaps you can come with me and do some sketches?" she asked, hopefully.

"That would be fun, but Kadin has invited Pyrra and I to Dubai for the weekend and I've always wanted to go there; especially since they've built the world's tallest building." The pair continued to discuss the trip to Dubai and Angus congratulated her on her competition win before other guests at the Gathering mingled in their direction.

It was not long before Godroi called them to order again.

"As with all young of any kind it is the adults that teach the ways of the species; how to act; what to do; what is right and what is wrong!" he looked around him at the audience. "You might expect this to fall on the parents, but as this is the first birth for many years we have appointed elders to guide the fire whelps in the more ancient of our ways. This ensures that our traditions do not falter nor dwindle from existence..."

This was the bit Angus was interested in and he could not wait to see whom Godroi had chosen for such an important task. He thought for a second that it might be Pyrra but since she had not mentioned it at all he did not think it was her.

"...and for that reason I have chosen one of our wiser and more revered number to take up this role!"

'This was it' thought Angus as he looked eagerly around the cavern. At a mention from Godroi a dragon at the back of the throng began to move forward and at first it was difficult to see who it was. After a few seconds Faris moved into view and Angus immediately smiled as that made perfect sense; but then Faris stepped aside to reveal a red dragon. The dragon was muttering and slowly made his way to the front where he stood not looking too impressed by the honour Godroi bestowed upon him. Angus stood with his mouth open in shock and quickly adjusted his features when Godroi started to clap. The young protector joined in with Godroi and as he did so he could see others start to do the same. The smattering of applause grew to a crescendo and Angus thought the Red dragon almost looked embarrassed at being the centre of attention. As everyone watched, the two young whelps bounded up to Macklin and immediately began to jump on him in a playful manner sensing that he was to become important in their young lives. Already Angus could see that their Heart Stones were glowing brightly and he noticed that they did not seem to be put off in the slightest by the gruff exterior of the Red dragon. In fact it appeared that he was smiling as he began to playfully push them down on the ground whilst tickling their bellies. 'Surely not!' thought Angus and, looking around, he could see that he was not the only one surprised by this and he was about to comment to Pyrra when he felt a tug at his elbow. He turned to see that Georgina had rejoined him. She looked at the red dragon and raised her eyebrows.

"Yeah I know; Macklin! I don't believe it either!" exclaimed Angus.

Chapter 5

'All in the Mind'

The two friends parted over England, both looking forward to their own adventures and secure in the knowledge that they would soon be seeing each other again. The flight from Krubera had been even more uneventful than usual and as they flew home Angus reflected what a brilliant day it had been for The Secret Society of Dragon Protectors. It was magnificent to see all the awakened dragons congregating together; yet another highlight of the Society's work so far. As normal Pyrra could sense that her young protector was deep in his own thoughts and she decided to join in the conversation that was no doubt taking place in his head.

"Well, what do you think of Macklin's new appointment then?" she asked.

"I wondered if Rathlin was going crazy!" laughed Angus. "I can't see Macklin being involved in the upbringing of the two young whelps; can you?"

"Well I must admit to being a little surprised but he did seem to take to the whelps and they him" she replied in an amused tone.

"Well, being around children will hopefully improve his temper" said Angus. "Remember what he was like in New York?"

As they flew on the duo recounted the tale of the grumpy dragon hiding in New York and the difficulties they had of finding him a new hiding place.

The week at school passed in a blur. Angus disliked the beginning of the Spring Term as it was still cold and dark in the mornings and he was never keen to leap out of bed on a weekday. After school he was mostly stuck indoors, either sorting stock or stuffing envelopes for his parents Kleanware business. If it was not that, it was delivering booklets through doors, and then it was the homework that the teachers piled on them after the school break. He counted the days to the weekend as this Friday held greater promise. It snowed constantly on Wednesday and Thursday and he and the other students received a note from the headmaster telling them that the school would be closed on Friday as it would be too dangerous to travel in the blizzard conditions forecast for the next two days. This meant he could go off to Dubai a day earlier than planned. Angus excused himself from his parents with a vague murmur about 'cabin fever' and having to go to see Rathlin and Aurora for the weekend, assuring them the weather had not reached that far north and that he could travel if he got away quickly.

"Are you sure it will be alright for you to travel up there Angus?" asked his mother as she fussed with his jacket and scarf.

"Yeah Mum it's fine and the weather seems to be better there anyway" he replied through the muffling of his scarf as he ran out of the front door.

Angus did not like to lie to his parents about where he was going as he knew this was fundamentally wrong; but to tell them the truth would mean telling them about the SSDP and apart from keeping the society's existence a secret it was best for them not to know. The end of the path neared and he tried to stop on the icy surface. As he slid to a grinding halt he wobbled out of control and narrowly missing braining himself on the gatepost. He turned and waved to his mum reassuringly and that was when he suddenly realised that if the roads were bad enough to close his school, he would not be able to get to Piggleston to meet Pyrra as they had planned. He walked a little further down the street and turned the corner carefully, stepping firmly on the icy pavement so as not to fall over again. He thought about what he could do to alert Pyrra and then he remembered that he had not had his discussion with Rathlin and Godroi about the strange things that had been happening to him. He had expected this to take place after the Joining ceremony but it had not transpired. A thought struck him and smiling to himself he headed for the Recreation Ground.

Angus stood in the small play park next to a large climbing frame shaped like a dome. It was bright orange but most of it was covered in snow and ice which gave it the eerie look of some enchanted icy palace. Concentrating his mind he thought hard of Pyrra, filling his mind with her image and willing her to come to him. He waited, standing completely still; but nothing happened. The chill began to numb his feet and he stamped them on the ground in an attempt to heat up. He knew he could not hang around forever and decided to have one last concerted effort. It was all he could do to focus on Pyrra as the cold began to bite into his skin. After about five minutes he was so cold that his teeth began to chatter and it was no longer possible for him to direct his thoughts to anything other than getting back to the warmth. He had just decided to leave when he realised that he was no longer feeling cold. His teeth had stopped chattering and he felt a rush of air beside him. The green dragon landed on the top of the domed climbing frame, stamping her feet at the unusual feeling of snow beneath them and sending showers of snow and ice from the bars. The whole sight was very impressive and he laughed as it looked like the dragon had smashed through the ceiling of the ice palace.

"I've always wanted to do that!" she smiled down at him as the steel frame groaned under the weight of a dragon.

"You got my message then!" he grinned and Pyrra nodded.

They were getting quite good at this tuning in to each other, a rare intuition between dragon and protector. Angus had first become aware of it during the Trials of the Cor Stan and the last time he had used it was when he was freefalling from Meredith's office block. He would most certainly had died from the impact of the fall, but his mind called out to Pyrra and she answered by flying to pluck him out of the air.

"No time to delay, jump up and let's get out of this freezing country and head for the sunshine of Dubai!" the dragon enthused.

Quick as a flash the lad climbed up the frame and onto her back.

Chapter 6

'The Water Dragon'

Soon the dragon gained height above the icy landscape below and soared into the snow heavy clouds just before the next downfall. Pyrra switched into dragon time which meant they could travel great distances much quicker, and Angus settled in for the ride. The roughly 3500 mile flight eastwards began quite uneventfully as they passed over the southern part of the British Isles and out over the English Channel. Angus looked around not really taking in where they were, but after they reached France he realised that he could recognise the area far below them.

"Pyrra, we are going to Dubai, right?" he asked carefully.

"Absolutely!" she replied.

She smiled at the silence that followed as she could almost hear his mind working.

"But this is the way we travel to Krubera?"

Pyrra turned her head slowly so that Angus could see that she was grinning at him.

"Well now. You would be correct on that..." she replied, "but you're assuming that Dubai is in the south when in fact it's in the south east and we have to almost pass over Krubera on the way to the Middle East and the Arabian Gulf." She added a wink at the end.

"Ok smarty-pants!" replied Angus. "It's okay for those that have a built in GPS in their head!" he grinned back at her.

Now that he had his geography sorted out by the dragon Angus left Pyrra to do the driving and he settled back, hypnotised by the rhythm of her beating wings until he fell asleep.

The rest of the journey passed quite uneventfully and remarkably quickly. The Black Sea was very cold at this time of year and he woke up briefly to pull his jacket and scarf into a better position. Pyrra's natural body heat protected him from the chilled wind and adverse elements. Quite soon Angus regretted wearing his warm fleece and scarf. After they had left the region of the Black Sea the temperature started to rise, and by the time they were over the northern Gulf he had to pull off his gloves and put them in his pocket. The Middle Eastern mid-day sun was strong and as they travelled further south it became warmer. To the left Angus could see a large mountainous region with snow caps as far as the eye could see. To his right were vast deserts and he guessed that the great Sahara was somewhere in that direction. Below him the sea was clear and blue and he noticed numerous structures in the water. At first he thought they might be ships but then he saw some were connected by thin bridges and that they were permanent. It was not until he saw the spouting flames from a flare tower that he realised they must be oil or gas rigs. Not for the first time he marvelled at how lucky he was to have such a unique vantage point from which to view the world. He was always thankful that he had met Pyrra, but at times like this he really did appreciate the benefits of dragon friendship.

They continued to follow the Arabian Gulf southwards and the desert land mass on the right began to extend in front of them. At first all Angus could see was a dusty haze in the distance, but as they neared land Angus spotted many islands with a backdrop of tall skyscrapers surrounded by numerous smaller white buildings. The islands began to form shapes and the group now nearest them appeared to be in the shape of a map of the world which Angus found really strange. A number of boats appeared to be spraying sandy water onto the islands and he wondered why they were doing it. Pyrra turned her head and pointed to a large tree shaped island in the clear blue sea.

"That must be The Palm!" shouted Angus. "Kadin told
me about it
They flew towards the enormous manmade island and in
the direction of the city.

Observing the mainland terrain below, Angus saw a
sprawling metropolis bisected with roads and flyovers; the
desert stretching as far as the eye could see into the haze
beyond. One of Dubai's most distinctive landmarks, Burj al
Arab towered below them; shaped like a huge white
billowing sail. The hotel was almost visible from the entire
Emirate as it stood alone, towering above the sandy
beaches which were now filled with sunbathers. Pyrra
swooped in for a closer view of the strange building and
Angus noticed that it had a helicopter landing pad on top.
He pointed to it and Pyrra decided to land there to get her
bearings and a welcome rest since she had been flying for
some time without a break. The truth was it had been the
longest journey she had attempted, being much further
than Krubera.

"Are you okay Pyrra?" asked Angus as he jumped from
her back onto the windswept helipad.

"Of course I am!" she replied smiling, "You don't need
to worry about me... now just look at this fantastic view!"

Pyrra had walked to the edge of the helipad and was peering over the edge. Angus took a minute to peel off some of his warmer clothing and stuff it into his backpack as the temperature was significantly higher in Dubai than it was in the snowy England they had left behind. He joined her to see that a safety net encircled the whole helipad and even in the daylight, various lights blinked on and off. He turned to look around and noticed a video surveillance camera sited at the entrance to the top of the building.

"Just as well we're invisible, eh?" he said to Pyrra, pointing to the doorway.

"What makes you think we are? I might have switched it off!" replied Pyrra looking serious.

"Then we had better go before the security guards and the police appear!" laughed Angus.

They quickly discussed the instructions provided by Kadin and after coming to an agreement as to the correct direction were soon ready for the last short leg of the journey.

Pyrra sprang from the heli-deck and immediately dove headlong down the side of the Burj. Angus eyes began to water due to the combination of the speed of their descent and the warm air. As was her normal style, Pyrra flicked her wings out and levelled out a few yards from the ground before she flew over the rooftops of the nearest hotel and houses. From this height Angus spied palm trees sprouting among a multitude of houses and a fun looking water park with big slides. These houses were not like the ones he was used to back home. Instead of red brick or dull grey weathered stonework these houses were mostly painted bright white or beige. The other thing that struck him was they appeared to be bigger than the houses back in the UK. As the houses swept underneath them they gave way to a highway with more lanes than Angus had seen on any road. Very fast flowing traffic raced along both sides of the road and if it had not been so straight he might have mistaken it for a race track. Alongside the highway was an elevated concrete structure with tracks and Angus watched as a sleek light blue train emerged from a shiny armadillo-shaped building that he assumed was a station. Pyrra turned slowly to follow the highway and Angus looked up to see that they were heading directly for the skyscrapers in the distance. As they travelled Angus heard a very unusual sound. At first it was difficult to make out but then it began to echo around and with them as they flew towards the heart of Dubai. Angus listened to the chanting words that appeared to come from all around them but he could not understand them and guessed that whoever was speaking must have been doing so in Arabic.

"Do you know exactly where we will meet Kadin and Nehebkau?" he asked Pyrra.

"We are aiming for the newest landmark... the one you really wanted to see!" replied Pyrra.
As she said this she pointed her snout forward as the world's tallest building loomed in front of them, rising high above the other tower blocks like a needle. Angus was speechless as he had actually thought that the building was much further away. Now that his mind registered its nearness, the scale of it really was very impressive, especially from the air. He could now see how much it dwarfed the neighbouring buildings and it was by far the tallest thing in the entire area and he was sure you would be able to see it for many miles.

"Can we fly around it Pyrra? We still have a little while before we need to meet Kadin" he asked, checking his watch.

"I thought you'd never ask!" she grinned back at him. The green dragon flicked her wings and sped towards the base of the massive building and began to sweep around it in a wide arc. Angus could see a large shallow lake filled with pipes that sat just under the surface of the water.

He wondered what they were for and he could even see some men in diving suits swimming around them and checking various parts. Pyrra changed direction and swept further up the glass and aluminium covered facade drawing Angus' attention back to their ascent. He looked inside some of the many windows and at this height he could see that many offices occupied the lower floors and what appeared to be hotel rooms. As they climbed further the building became thinner and the tiers became smaller. It took them several minutes and several revolutions around the spire, but eventually they reached the top and Angus was surprised to see dozens of people inside one of the levels quite near the top. They were on the viewing deck of the building and busily taking pictures and video footage of the splendid views the world's tallest building offered. None of the people inside were aware that hovering just outside the windows were a 2000 year old dragon and a 13 year old boy!

Pyrra circled back down towards the lake and touched down on a roof terrace in the shadow of Burj Khalifa. Angus had barely slid from her back when he heard a familiar voice welcome them. He turned to see Kadin in his sparkling white khandoura, running up the stairs.

"As-salaam alaykum" said Kadin greeting him in Arabic.

"Hi Kadin, how are you?" replied Angus resolving to learn the proper reply before the end of this trip.

"I trust you had a good journey Angus my friend and I'm sorry if I kept you waiting. I have been to the Mosque with my father and could only just get away" explained Kadin.

"We landed just before you arrived" replied Angus. "We decided to do a little bit of sightseeing."

"Indeed. I saw both of you flying around the Burj... I should really do that myself with Nehebkau!" replied Kadin thoughtfully.

"We couldn't resist it and I wasn't expecting to see all those people up there!" added Angus.

"Oh yes, you can go to viewing deck near the top in the express elevator and take in the views, but it's better from the back of a dragon; don't you think?" replied Kadin grinning.

"Where is Nehebkau?" asked Pyrra looking for the Asian dragon that Kadin protected.

"In shaa'Allah, we'll see him soon... he can be a bit lazy on a Friday... it's our weekend you know" laughed Kadin. "Come, let's get something to eat... you must be hungry after your flight and Pyrra you surely need to rest."

"Indeed I do!" she yawned.

As the boys left, Pyrra folded her wings around her and lay down on the terrace enjoying the warmth of the tiles against her skin. Angus knew she would be quite safe being invisible to all but possessors of Dragonore. He took a moment to remove his sweatshirt, leaving him with his t-shirt whilst Pyrra basked in the late afternoon sunshine.

Kadin busied himself with a menu and after a few moments a waiter brought fresh mango juice to drink and a selection of Arabic mezze for them to eat. Kadin insisted that Angus tried everything from the hummus and olives with pita bread; to kibbeh, moutabal, tabbouleh and fattoush and since he was ravenous this did not pose any problems for him. When the food arrived garnished with brightly coloured pickles Angus enjoyed the new savoury tastes whilst catching up with his Arabic friend.

"I can't believe how nice the weather is here..." said Angus through a mouthful of chicken kebab.

"Yes it is colder at this time of year but the midday sun is very pleasant" replied Kadin seriously.

"This is cold? You're lucky! It was so cold in England I could hardly stay outside for more than 10 minutes!" laughed Angus.

Kadin went on to explain to Angus that the chanting noise he heard all over the city was the 'call to prayer' and that it was coming from every mosque in the city, announcing Prayer Time at various hours of the day. They continued to discuss the culture of Dubai and Angus quizzed Kadin on some of the phrases he used when they first met. After a while they finished eating and Angus could see that it was already beginning to get dark.

"I must have lost track of time, is it that late already?" he said.

"It is nearly 6pm my friend, but here our sunrise and sunset are very much the same all year. Being nearer the

Equator we do not have the same daylight issues you have in Europe.

"I guess I expected it to be like our summertime since it was so sunny" replied Angus, and added "by the way where's Pyrra?" when he realised she was no longer on the terrace and nowhere to be seen.

The boys looked around anxiously and things were made all the more difficult with the promenade filling up with so many people. Something seemed to be happening and Angus hoped it was nothing to do with his best friend.

After a long nap the green dragon was curious about this new place she had come to and, thinking she would not be missed, went off to explore on her own. After inspecting some of the buildings in the area, which included a massive multi-storey car park; she was intrigued when she suddenly heard a burst of loud music. Crowds of humans had gathered around the lake at the base of the world's tallest building and Pyrra could not resist finding out why. As the sun dipped over the horizon large fountains sprang into life. She was delighted as the music increased in volume and tempo and amazed when jets of water started shooting skyward in time to the rhythm. 'Argent would love this' she thought. The fountain display lasted a few minutes and the music reached a huge crescendo with the fountains shooting water high into the air like gun fire. As suddenly as it started the fountain fell silent and the crowds started to move away. Pyrra was feeling rather warm after lying in the afternoon sunshine. After a little while the crowds gathered again at the best viewing places on the terracing around the lake. She decided she would watch and wait.

"Pyrra... there you are!" called Angus from another terrace. "I'm coming over!"
She watched the two lads run through the crowd and up the stairs to the spot she had chosen to view the wonderful spectacle from.

"How was dinner then?" she asked as Angus arrived panting.

"The food was great... but I was a bit worried when you were not where we left you!" he replied.

"Well I'm a big girl you know... I can look after myself!" she grinned. "I've discovered this wonderful fountain and I think it might be about to start again."

"Yes it will" said Kadin, "it plays every 30 minutes, different types of music in the evenings and it's very popular."

"I can see why..." she replied, "It looks very inviting!"

Angus could sense she was up to something and he had an idea what it was.

"Now Pyrra we don't want to draw attention to ourselves so just stop whatever it is you're thinking!" he warned.

His attempt to rein in his friend was all in vain. No sooner had he said that, than the music started and Pyrra just could not help herself. She launched off the steps of the terrace, swooped towards the water just as the fountain cycle started again.

"Oh no!" said Kadin in dismay.

The fountains water jets danced to a different tune this time and it was even livelier than before. Angus watched as Pyrra flew in and out of the water jets and it reminded him of the training they did at Long Reach. Higher and faster went the water as Pyrra danced around them wings outstretched, cooling off after her long flight. This time the Burj Khalifa sparkled brilliantly in the background as hundreds of lights flashed in various sequences, up and down the tall tower. The fountain also danced on longer than before, but unlike the last time it did not finish with a volley of water shots into the air. Instead the tune culminated in a cacophony of musical noise which was accompanied with the biggest wall of water Angus had ever seen. The water literally fanned hundreds of feet into the air; and into Pyrra!

The watching crowd collectively gasped in delight and that was the moment when the boys realised that they were not the only ones to see the dragon. They were horrified as Pyrra's shape was perfectly outlined. The water had not only bounced off of her, but it had wrapped around the dragon's invisible body to reveal the solid

shape that was normally hidden to all but a dragon protector. An excited mutter went around the crowd as everyone stared at the silhouette of a great water dragon with wings outstretched and

perfectly illuminated for all to see!

Chapter 7

'Vanishings'

Georgina's school was open on Friday as the bad weather had not reached that far west, but she had been given the day off to research Kew Gardens for the Teenage Guide she had been chosen to write. She was wrapped up warmly against the winter cold as she entered through the big iron gates. Her father had been taking her to the Royal Botanical Gardens at Kew ever since she was a little girl, but this was her first visit on her own and she had a task to do. This made Georgina very happy and the fact that she had won a competition to earn this privilege made it all the more satisfying. Even though she knew the place very well she studied a map of the layout on a large board just inside the entrance and worked out a route, keeping notebook and pen in her gloved hand so she could jot down anything of interest as she went along. Georgina took a deep breath and filled her lungs with crisp winter air and exhaled, watching the steam. It was very cold indeed, but no snow had fallen in this area of London as yet; although the sky looked heavy with it. Kew was one of the most famous public gardens in the world, but Georgina was disappointed to see that there was not much by way of colour in the flower beds at this time of year, but she enjoyed the brisk walk and the sight of bright red berries on the bushes as the birds enjoyed feasting on them. Inside the glasshouses however, there was plant life in abundance. She spied a large glass structure and headed indoors, seeking warmth. There in the Princess of Wales Conservatory, Georgina enjoyed discovering the different climates for growing cacti and alpines and was fascinated by the carnivorous Venus flytrap plants. She watched these plants actually close up as if devouring flies they had lured into their leafy jaws and made a few notes in her book, knowing this would be something the readers of her guide would not want to miss. Once back outside she walked along a straight path to the Palm House and jotted down that it was a marvellous Victorian hothouse full of exotic plants bearing strange fruits, with wrought iron spiral staircases right up into the roof and a wonderful tropical steamy atmosphere that smelled of peat; a giant greenhouse.

Out through the back door and in the cold once more Georgina pulled on her gloves and headed for a tiny round glass house and turned the old brass door knob which was a bit stiff, and she shouldered it open. She was delighted to find within, giant green lily pads from South America which filled a round pond, which in turn, filled the small circular building with just enough room to walk around the edge. Georgina had never seen such huge water lily leaves and they gave the impression that they would take your weight if you walked across them. Being winter, the water lilies themselves were not yet in bloom. Spying another glasshouse, Georgina headed for the warmth of the Temperate House, home of the world's largest indoor plant, and sat down on a bench making sure each of these interesting features were jotted down and underlined in her very neat handwriting. The diligent girl was pleased with the progress she had made and was reluctant to leave the pleasant climate of the glasshouse. Setting off along the path she saw a bus stop for the 'Kew Explorer' and decided to ride on the small shuttle bus which would take her further into the gardens, and save her legs. The Explorer came almost at once and there were only two other passengers. Tom, the driver, was very knowledgeable and told his small but rapt audience a potted history of the world famous gardens as they motored around the wide paths. Georgina enjoyed the rest and she sat up and took great interest when the pagoda came into view through a clearing. The pagoda was one of Kew's most famous buildings and seemed out of place in this setting, with its Eastern look...as if it had been stuck there as no one knew where else to put it. It was a reddish tower looking like it had been constructed out of building blocks. It appeared quite fragile, dwarfed by the trees and Georgina thought, quite recently painted. It put her in mind of the miniature oriental gardens her father used to make in his greenhouse, using cacti and small alpines for trees, and bits of mirror to make a lake spanned by tiny bridges, with gravel areas broken up by crazy paving paths and sometimes a model pagoda or panda. The tiny gardens would be planted in earthenware bowls and stored on shelves in his greenhouse to be sold at the village fete and Georgina had always been fascinated by these popular and fascinating creations; each one different. Tom's voice broke into her thoughts;

"This octagonal tower was built in 1762 when people in England were just finding out for the first time about the Orient due to recent exploration and were particularly curious about Chinese culture... pagodas such as this one became fashionable and Kew's was the tallest reconstruction of a pagoda in Europe at the time of building. It is built to a specific mathematic equation with each floor being 30cm less in height and diameter than the previous one giving an upwardly tapering effect. This pagoda has recently been restored..." Tom announced with great pride. He went on, "When the pagoda was erected it was brightly coloured and had varnished iron roof tiles and there were golden dragon figures guarding every corner of the eight sided building, on each of the ten storeys". 'Wow', thought Georgina, suddenly very interested indeed 'that's a lot of dragons!'

"What happened to the ornamental dragons? Where are they now, being restored?" she asked Tom.

"Nobody knows for sure, miss" the driver replied, pleased to have a keen audience, "Eighty dragons just vanished...and haven't been mentioned in the records since Hanoverian times." He leant forward and lowered his voice, speaking behind his hand directly to Georgina;

"Although some say King George IV sold them off to clear his debts... because the Gardens belonged to the Crown in those days and golden dragon statues must have been worth something. I think the dragon statues were wooden but covered in pure gold leaf. I remember them talking about making some replicas about thirty years ago but nothing ever came of that plan"

Georgina made some notes and closed her notebook, satisfied with her research, and got off the Kew Explorer in need of a hot drink. She went into the coffee shop and bought a steaming mug of hot chocolate piled high with whipped cream, and a cheese sandwich to eat, and sat down to review her notes and study the map for anything she'd missed. Georgina was the only customer in the café and she enjoyed her late lunch in solitude, reading through the notes she had made and pleased with her morning's accomplishments. She saw on the map something labelled 'The Queen's Beasts' flanking the Palm House and decided to go back to have a look at them, having missed them previously by coming out of the glasshouse by the back entrance. The Queen's Beasts turned out to be an

impressive line of statues depicting heraldic beasts representing Queen Elizabeth II's royal lineage sculpted in stone after her Coronation and donated to Kew in the 1950's. Georgina spotted a dragon statue straight away, but her Dragonore remained cold so she knew nothing was hiding in it at that time.

There was also a gryphon, a unicorn, a yale; which she'd

never heard of before and turned out to be a type of spotted antelope. She also found a falcon, a horse and a bull as well as two lions and a white greyhound making ten in all. It crossed her mind how amazing it would be if these other mythical creatures were also hibernating in their likenesses and she wondered if perhaps they were, but that no one had found the key yet. Then she decided she was just being silly, but imagine if there really were unicorns and gryphons hiding in statues and not just dragons! All the beasts had their backs to the Palm House which she presumed they were supposed to be guarding, whilst looking out over the picturesque lake and fountain.

Jumping up from the bench, Georgina glanced at her watch and replaced the lid on her pen. She just had time to find the Treetop Walkway near the Temperate House, one of the garden's newest attractions. She was exhilarated by the sensation of climbing and counted each of the 118 wooden steps to the top and then edged onto the walkway itself, peering down through the leaves of the trees and seeing the gardens from an entirely different angle 18 meters up off the ground. Georgina took in all the different colours of the winter foliage and wished Angus was with her to sketch the panoramic view. The walkway spanned some 200 meters and she knew teenage visitors would not want to miss this so she paused to make notes for her pamphlet, leaning her book on the handrail. As the afternoon wore on Georgina felt the air temperature drop and she stamped her feet to keep warm, replacing her notebook in her bag she descended the wooden staircase to return to the gate to wait for her father as arranged, making sure to take a quick look at the exhibition beneath the walkway which explained how trees grow. It was just after 4:30 in the afternoon and already dark. Georgina heard approaching footsteps and started to turn to greet her father with a smile.

"Daddy, did you know there used to be dra..." Suddenly she was plunged into complete darkness and she struggled to remove something that was covering her face. Someone else grabbed her arms and pinned them to her body. As she tried to scream out for help but a large hand clamped over her mouth and muffled her voice before she could utter a sound. An unfamiliar voice growled into her ear.

"Now don't you worry little lady just you co-operate... the boss just wants a word with you."
The horror of her situation was all too much and as the panic rose in her mind, Georgina gave in to the blackness.

Chapter 8

'The Emperor's New Clothes'

Angus and Kadin looked around at the crowd and almost as one they pulled out their mobile phones and started filming the dragon shape in the fountain.

"Tell me you got that on camera Bill?" said an American woman near to Angus whose husband had been filming the show with his camcorder.

The water had almost drained away from Pyrra, but nonetheless the very solid shape of a dragon body was seen by the watching crowd. Everyone pointed and discussed the sight with great interest and the noise of the crowd increased. Angus and Kadin were worried about the SSDP and Pyrra's safety; especially if the authorities took it seriously and started to investigate the incident.

"Clever isn't it, how they manage to do that..." said Kadin loudly, thinking on his feet.

At first Angus stared at him, wondering what his Arab friend was talking about, but then it dawned on him.

"Yeah... Tell me how they do that again!" he asked very loudly indeed so everyone around could hear.

"It's the latest computer technology you know... my Father's company commissioned it directly from

Hollywood..." replied Kadin acting out his part extremely well.

Angus noticed they had the attention of everyone around them. Some blatantly listened and others pretended not to, but everyone within earshot now heard their conversation.

"It looks like a real dragon!" he added for good measure.

"Yes, it's amazing what they can do with lasers these days..." finished Kadin with a grin.

After a few anxious moments word spread among the crowd about the fantastic special effects at the Dubai Fountains, the biggest and best in the world, with the outline of a dragon appearing right in the middle! It appeared that Kadin's ruse had worked and the boys slipped away to find Pyrra hopeful that no one would think that the dragon was actually real. The crowd were further distracted about the fountain incident when the light show started on the tall building. Sparkling lights danced up and down the building illuminating various parts of the building and wowing the spectators below.

Angus managed to summon Pyrra and the dragon had no idea of the rumpus she had caused. Angus tried to explain to her that invisibility does not work with water.

"Do you remember what happened when Nathair dived into Loch Ness?" Angus admonished as he tried to make her realise the crisis they had just averted. "He was showing off and pretending to be the Loch Ness Monster and although no one could see him, they certainly saw the ripples he made when he was messing around in the water" he explained to a very amused Kadin.

"Ah" was all she could say, "I didn't think about that; sorry!"

"No harm done" said Kadin, "come on I'll take you to my home... it's probably safer for you there Pyrra... as long as you promise not to dive into the swimming pool!" he laughed.

"Would it be okay if I just cooled off a little in it?" asked Pyrra half seriously.

"No offense but it's just been re-filled and you would probably empty it!"

Angus burst out laughing which did not amuse Pyrra.

"Sorry but the look on your face" he explained.

"Yes, well, no one likes to hear that they are too big!" she huffed.

Kadin felt embarrassed at insulting her and he apologised profusely, but she smiled and had to admit that she would be slightly larger than the average swimmer so she understood. This sent Angus into convulsions again and this time Pyrra joined in, having seen the funny side.

Kadin directed Pyrra as she flew the two boys away from the Burj Khalifa and along a road running next to the sea.

"That's it Pyrra, just follow the beach road along to the Palm!" shouted Kadin as he sat in front of Angus. They continued back the way Angus and Pyrra had flown earlier that afternoon, and Angus noticed a helicopter was landing on the Burj Al Arab just as they flew past. The bright lights of Palm Island shone just beyond the Burj. He could see cars streaming on and off the main highway to the Palm, all following the main boulevard with its fancy street lights sporting a blue light on top of the poles. At Kadin's direction Pyrra banked left from the Palm and flew over a large boundary wall. A massive entrance gate split the wall to the right of Angus. They joined the road behind the gate and continued up a palm tree lined driveway to alight on a large grass lawn.

Both boys jumped from Pyrra's back and Angus was struck dumb by the size of the house before him. It was huge and rivalled Meredith's mansion which he had visited on a couple of occasions. No-one was around, and as they walked toward the house, Angus spotted a massive garage off to one side. A man was busy washing two sports cars parked outside the garage and he noticed the equally jaw dropping collection of cars parked inside the garage.

"Exactly how rich is your Dad?" asked Angus, smiling.

"I don't know, but he has many businesses here in the UAE and abroad..." replied Kadin frankly, "One day he tells me it will all be mine; but for now I am happy being a dragon protector."

They had continued up the white marble entrance stairs to the large front door and Angus stepped into the most lavish hallway he could ever imagine. It was like something he had only seen on television when they show you the inside of a home that belonged to a famous movie star. Marble was very much the material in use and different colours adorned the hallway floor and walls. In front of him was a large split stairway that swept up each wall and met at a first floor landing. The whole thing was edged by an elaborate white marble balustrade, with the steps covered in plush carpet. Above him was an enormous golden chandelier; dripping in crystal and brilliantly lit by numerous small bulbs. Adorning the walls were many paintings which reminded Angus of Calmor. He marvelled at the paintings of racehorses in the hallway and the smart looking Arab gentlemen whose painting graced the stairs. On seeing the look of awe on his friends face, Kadin smiled.

"My father has many racehorses and he taught me to ride when I was very small. Of course now I prefer to ride dragons, but he doesn't know about that" the boy laughed.

"This place is awesome!" was all Angus could say in reply.

"We call this area the 'Majalis' or meeting place... do you mind waiting here a moment as my parents are keen to meet my English visitor?" said Kadin indicating a room off to one side of the hallway.

Angus nodded that he was fine and sat down on one of several identical sofas that lined the walls of the room. Various cushions lay on the floor which was covered by a very finely woven rug. The rug itself must have been twice the size of his parent's living room floor back home.

A little while later Kadin returned with his mother and father and they sat down to chat for a while before being called to supper.

"So Kadin tells me that you are a member of this animal conservation foundation he has got himself involved in?" asked Kadin's father with interest.

"Erm... yes!" Angus looked at Kadin for help, but the boy just sat looking innocent. "He joined a little while after I did and... we became good friends!" replied Angus with only the merest of pauses.

Kadin grinned at him and Angus knew that his Arab mate was having a bit of fun at his expense. He decided to play along.

"Of course he still has a lot to learn, but he's getting there!" added Angus.

That wiped the grin off of Kadin's face as his father turned his attention to his son.

"I hope you are paying attention and trying your best!" said his father sternly.

"Of course father. It is extremely important to me" replied Kadin suddenly serious now that the focus was back on him.

Soon they were ushered to supper outside in an outdoor Majalis and the boys grinned at each other as they followed his parents out of the house.

The whole of Kadin's family were in the Majalis which was open to the night sky. Again Angus enjoyed more Arabic hospitality, and afterwards the women and smaller children left to go inside as Kadin's father smoked sheesha from an ornate pipe he shared with some other men. Whilst the adults reclined on large cushions and discussed the matters of the day; Angus watched and enjoyed the fruity aroma. He was not offered any to try though and he did not think he would, knowing it was tobacco. He looked up at the night sky and wondered how many constellations he recognised.

"The sky is so clear here" he said to Kadin.

"Just wait until we go out into the desert tomorrow..." said Kadin, "we're going to sleep out under the stars and the night sky is much clearer out there away from the bright lights of the city".

Angus could not wait to see that and after excusing himself from the others he bade Pyrra goodnight. The dragon, exhausted from her flight and fountain adventures, curled up unseen in the courtyard to sleep, with a smile on her face. Kadin escorted Angus upstairs to an enormous guest bedroom which had the biggest flat screen television Angus had ever seen. He succumbed to sleep in the huge bed after what had been a very long and eventful day. The memories of Pyrra's dance in the fountain faded with the smile on his face as the blue dragon began to invade his mind again.

The next morning Angus awoke early to the call to prayer he had heard when they arrived in the Emirate the previous day. He looked out of the window to see Pyrra had also woken up at the unfamiliar musical sound. Angus washed and went looking for Kadin, but the lad's bedroom door was ajar and he was not there. He decided not to wait and got dressed in far fewer clothes than he had worn the previous morning and slipped downstairs and outside to speak to Pyrra.

"That was a good night's sleep last night, the temperature was perfect... I think I might move here!" she said, but after seeing the look on Angus' face. "Of course I'm only joking... A holiday might be good though."

"We might be able to manage that I think" he replied, visibly relieved.

The pair waited on the lawn and soaked up the early morning sun until Kadin returned from the Mosque. After that they breakfasted on warm flat bread, milk sweetened with honey and a few fresh dates.

"Come my friends, let us meet with Nehebkau; Pyrra, may I direct you?" announced Kadin at the end of the meal.

Pyrra nodded her agreement, although in truth she was enjoying the taste of the dates. However as good as they were dates were no substitute for her favourite cough candies and Angus knowing his best friend all too well, recognised the look on her face and surreptitiously slipped a sweet from his pocket sweet into her mouth. The happy dragon took off from the garden carrying both boys, and flew out over the wall towards the city centre. They did not follow the highway this time but instead Kadin pointed them diagonally towards an extremely fancy looking building that stood alone in the desert.

"That looks like a giant bird" he said to Kadin.

"I am sure the designer would be pleased to hear you say that Angus as that is exactly what it should look like!" answered Kadin over his shoulder. "It is the Meydan race course and a place my father loves to visit as often as business will allow."

Angus looked at the vast layout of the place and could only wonder at the size. As they passed further over Dubai Kadin pointed to another white roofed building that sat on the edge of the desert. From this height Angus could see that the building was shaped like an enormous white dragon.

"Here we are!" announced Kadin triumphantly.

He guided Pyrra to the front entrance of the shopping mall known as Dragon Mart. The building itself was not only shaped like a huge dragon but it also had dragons placed around it in various locations. They came down to land near the 'head' end of the building, by a large golden replica of a globe and wrapped around it was a magnificent

green dragon. It stood
in the middle of a pool
surrounded by smaller
dragons and Angus
could not decide if they
were dancing around
the globe or standing
in worship. Either way
the fountain did not
appear to be working.

"I hope you are not
going to jump in Pyrra" said Kadin, grinning at her.
Both boys fell about laughing at their joke, as the edges of
the green dragon statue started to blur and Nehebkau
morphed out from his hiding place.

It was still early in the morning and the shopping centre
was not yet open so there were not many people around.
The two dragons exchanged news, much as the boys had
done the day before. Angus and Kadin sat on a bench and
planned the rest of the day; a visit to the indoor ski slope
and then barbeque and camp in the desert. Angus was
very excited by the plans and could not wait to get into the
desert.

"So that's today sorted... what about tomorrow?" asked Angus, eager to make the most of his trip.

Suddenly both dragons looked skyward and Angus knew immediately something was wrong as he felt it too.

"What is it Pyrra?" he asked, but he already knew that another dragon was approaching.

A blue dot appeared on the horizon advancing towards them rather rapidly and at first Angus was taken aback as the colour reminded him of the dragon from his recent dreams! 'Would he finally be meeting him?' he wondered. As the dragon got nearer it became more recognisable as Georgina's dragon, Wymarc.

Chapter 9

'Bad News From Home'

The exhausted blue dragon collapsed in a heap next to the fountain and Pyrra was greatly concerned for her friend as he tried to speak.

"Please Wymarc drink some water..." she urged as she ushered him to the pool.

Wymarc drank for what seemed like ages to Angus. The lad knew something bad had happened, or the dragon would not be here. At last Wymarc lifted his head from the water.

"What is it?" asked Angus urgently, fearing the worst.

"Georgina has gone missing!" replied the dragon delivering his shocking news.

"What do you mean missing?" asked Pyrra, noting Angus' silence.

"We fear she may have been kidnapped... Her father and Rathlin have been out with the City Guardians trying to find her" he finished, still panting heavily.

Angus was stunned and could think of nothing to say. He knew she was in trouble and his heart felt heavy with regret that he was not around to protect her. His emotions welled up in his chest so much that he felt he was going to explode and it was all he could do just to maintain his composure in front of his friends.

"Where and when did this happen?" probed Pyrra.

"She was last seen at Kew Gardens... to the south west of London, but she failed to meet her father at the gate as planned... It's all my fault... I should have been with her!" replied poor Wymarc, blaming himself.

"No Wymarc... she is your protector, not the other way round" said Angus, finally mastering his emotions.

"It works both ways you know" Pyrra reminded him wisely.

Angus thought of all the times she had saved his life and nodded his agreement to her.

"Can you tell us anything else?" asked Angus.

"Not much... all they found was her notebook and pen outside the gate... It was on the ground and there were signs of a struggle" replied Wymarc.

"No witnesses?" asked Pyrra.

"None... and when our search was failing to turn anything up I said we should let you know, but Hugh and Rathlin told me you would be unable to do anything so best to leave you to enjoy your holiday for now" answered the dragon, still looking exhausted.

"Kadin, I need to talk to Rathlin... did you bring your mobile?" asked Angus, jumping to his feet.

Kadin felt the pocket of his dishdash.

"No sorry, I must have left it at home; we will need to go back."

The group flew back to Kadin's home in Al Sufouh utterly dejected by the news of Georgina's disappearance. They trailed a remorseful and very tired Wymarc in their wake and Angus hardly noticed the journey as he was lost in his own thoughts. 'Who would want to kidnap Georgina?' and 'Why hadn't anyone contacted him; did they not think he had a right to know?" His anxiety for Georgina was quickly being replaced by anger.

The three dragons touched down on the vast lawn at Kadin's villa and both boys ran to the house to get the mobile. They sprinted up the stairs two at a time and into Kadin's bedroom on the first floor. As Kadin searched for his mobile Angus noticed the desk by the window had a computer sitting on it with the power indicator flashing to signify it was in sleep mode. A thought struck Angus and he walked to the desk.

"Kadin can I borrow your laptop for a second?" he asked.

"Of course my friend... but don't you want to call Rathlin first?" answered Kadin, confused by the sudden change in direction.

"I do want to call him, but I just need to check on something and it will only take a minute" replied Angus mysteriously.

Once on the Internet, Angus quickly found the news site he was looking for and searched for the first person he would consider to be responsible for Georgina's disappearance. The article on Meredith Quinton-Jones flashed up on the screen and he was not disappointed. He had read about her the week before and the latest report on her court business confirmed that she had indeed been released with all charges suspended. It appeared that after the incident at the Natural History Museum her lawyers had successfully had her released on medical grounds and although she was still on probation she was free to go about her normal life.

"Do you think she has anything to do with Georgina's disappearance?" asked Kadin, having just read the article over Angus' shoulder.

Angus noticed another article which was dated a day later than the one he had been reading and he clicked on it with the mouse. The new article mentioned that she was returning to work and Meredith was quoted as saying 'I am now getting the help I require after my episode and am looking forward to getting back to work. I intend to visit my overseas companies as soon as possible'.

"I do now!" he replied sternly.

Angus closed the laptop and took the proffered phone from a worried looking Kadin. He rang Calmor forgetting the time difference and paced up and down the room as he waited on the line connecting. It was very early in the morning in Scotland, but he need not have worried as both Rathlin and Aurora Tek had not had much sleep. They had been up all night checking in with various protectors and dragons on the search network they had setup to find Georgina.

"Hi Rathlin, its Angus!" said Angus down the phone as soon as the head of the SSDP answered.

"Angus how a..."

"Have you found Georgina yet?" asked Angus cutting off Rathlin mid sentence.

Normally the lad would not have been that rude, but Rathlin understood how much Georgina meant to him and considering the circumstances he ignored the infringement.

"No... Not yet..." was the dejected answer, "and I guess we can call the search off for Wymarc as I now know he is with you in Dubai!"

"Yes he is and I'm glad he came... you should have called me Rathlin!" replied Angus, the anger he felt earlier welling up inside again.

"We wanted to my boy, but I was afraid you would be so upset as to try and get back too quickly and cause you or Pyrra some harm!" he replied gravely. "To be honest I had thought we would have her back by now but that hope is lost now!"

"What do you mean?" asked Angus, suddenly concerned again.

"Well the police have said that normally they would find someone within few hours, but it's already taken too long and..." his voiced wavered and trailed off.
Angus realised how upset the others would be as they too felt a lot for Georgina. They saw her as family and his anger quelled slightly.

"I'm sorry Rathlin... I'm sure you've done all you can" said Angus, "what is happening now?"

"The police are still making enquiries but we have started our own nationwide search using the SSDP network."

"Any sign of her?" asked Angus eagerly.

"Nothing I'm afraid... it's as if she has disappeared off the face of the planet, but I'm positive we will find her!" he replied half-heartedly.

Angus fell silent as he thought about the article and Rathlin's last comment. Rathlin knew these silences all too well.

"What's on your mind lad?" he asked cautiously.

"Georgina's disappearance might be something to do with Meredith" answered Angus.

"How can you say that Angus; do you have proof?"

"Think about it Rathlin, it makes sense... Who else would go to the bother of kidnapping her?"

Rathlin realised that Angus had a point and if he was honest the thought had crossed his own mind.

"I considered that as well but she was in jail and I don't think she would risk such a thing" replied Rathlin.

"I just checked the Web and she's been released... she's even been quoted as going overseas to attend to business!" said Angus.

"I didn't know that lad" replied Rathlin sounding thoughtful, "still, it doesn't mean she is responsible..."

"Come on Rathlin, she's taken Georgina to get back at me..." said Angus cutting in again, "and she will have taken her overseas, I'm sure of it... She won't risk staying in Britain, not after the court case and we need to go and track her down!"

"Now lad just slow down for a second or two and think about this rationally!" replied Rathlin, "you don't know anything for sure and it is no good running off to accuse anyone without some proof!"

Angus never answered as he knew what was coming next.

"I know you're hurting lad but we need to be sure. Now let me check things out at this end and I will get back to you. In the meantime you stay put and don't come home until you planned to; okay?"

"Yeah, okay" replied Angus sharply after a moment's pause.

Chapter 10

'Not Much of a Choice'

Georgina had been forcefully pulled along a path.
During her ordeal she had managed to work out that a
hood had been placed over her head when she was first
taken. She had no idea where she was now as she had
fainted during the struggle, but when she recovered she
had spent several hours in an uncomfortable box with her
hands bound behind her back and with no food or water. It
seemed a very long time since the hot chocolate at Kew!
During her journey Georgina could hear the sound of wind
and guessed that she had perhaps been flown
somewhere, but by what means she did not know and
apart from that she knew nothing else about her journey.
Since then she had been manhandled along what felt like a
rough track or road. Having been denied her sight for so
long she had relied on her other senses to determine more
about her situation. She had heard muffled voices talking
ahead of her but had been unable to make any sense of
what they said. Her nose detected a smell of vegetation,
like trees or bushes of some kind so she guessed they
were in the countryside and not in a city. It was also cold,
in fact very cold; much colder than at Kew, and her

instincts told her that she was in a different country. The two men that escorted her had not spoken much, but one had a rough heavy voice and the other had difficulty breathing as if his sinuses were blocked. Suddenly they stopped walking and she was spun around to face the direction they had just come. A hand was placed on her shoulder, the hood pulled off her head and the sudden burst of light felt like it would penetrate through her very skull.

Hands still bound behind her Georgina blinked in the bright sunlight. She dropped her head and rolled it to try and avoid looking at the light directly and to gain clarity as quickly as possible. Her head hurt from the sunlight and it took a few moments for her to be able to focus properly. As her vision cleared she tried to ascertain exactly where she was. Georgina's first impression was that she was quite high up as she was surrounded by snow covered hills and mountains. However they stood in a valley and there were the remnants of snow on the ground. The trees she could smell earlier were off to one side of the valley and in the distance she could see a structure or a road that somehow appeared familiar. She looked at the two men standing next to her and could not really make them out as both wore hooded coats that were zipped up against the cold.

She could hear voices talking behind her but they were too far away to hear them properly and when she tried to turn around the two men tightened their grip on her arms to stop her. The voices got louder as did the footsteps and she guessed they were coming towards her. She closed her eyes and focusing on her hearing again, listened to what was apparently the end of a conversation.

".... expect we will find out once we put her in; won't we!" said a woman's voice.

She recognised the voice immediately, one she knew very well, and her heart sank.

"Ah, Miss Penfold... apologies for the discomfort, but I am sure a bright girl like you will realise the need for secrecy" said Meredith Quinton-Jones as the she strode in front of the captive girl.

A chill ran through Georgina's body that had nothing to do with the air temperature. She stood motionless, her head reeling with dark thoughts and despair as she found herself staring into the cold green eyes of Meredith.

"What... nothing to say?" mocked the dark haired woman, "How very unlike you... but then, this must have come as a nasty shock to you, so I will forgive you this time."

The young protector wanted to scream at the hateful woman in front of her but Georgina's emotions were torn between absolute anger to abject fear and she could not speak. Her eyes welled with tears of frustration and in apprehension of what her captor would do to her.

"Now, now my dear, we don't want any of this now, do we?" said Meredith using her thumb to wipe a solitary tear from Georgina's left cheek. "We need you to be strong, don't we?"

The mockery was too much and defiance welled up within Georgina.

"Don't touch me you evil witch!" replied Georgina through gritted teeth.

"That's the spirit!" said Meredith stepping back and grinning smugly, "Now I expect you will be all defiance and stubbornness now, but you will soon change your attitude" added the disgraced former member of the Secret Society of Dragon Protectors.

Clearly the woman wanted some form of revenge, but whatever it was Georgina felt she was in grave danger from the deranged woman.

At a nod from Meredith, Georgina felt her bonds being loosened and she rubbed the circulation back into her wrists.

"Where am I? And why have you brought me here?" asked the girl, with a false air of courage as she certainly did not feel very brave on the inside.

"I don't think you are in a position to be asking any questions!" said another voice from behind her. Georgina's eyes widened incredulously as Felspar walked from behind her to stand behind Meredith. The black dragon sneered maliciously at the girl's shock as she, like the rest of the SSDP, had assumed him dead.

"Yes girly... As you can see I'm proving to be rather indestructible!" he growled.

Faced with the two most despised beings ever to come into contact with Georgina and the SSDP, the young protector's mind swam. Her legs felt like jelly and if it were not for the two guards holding her arms, she would have collapsed there and then.

"Yes, well anyway you are here now and I have a little job for you..." continued Meredith, "it won't take long if you co-operate and be a good little girl."

Meredith waved her hand and the two men spun the limp girl around. Led by the wayward oil executive they trudged further up the track and turned off into a densely overgrown area of trees and bushes. They had to walk in single file as there was only had a narrow path to walk on.

As they had walked Georgina had regained her composure somewhat and was now thinking about escape. She was calculating if she would be able to disappear into the bushes before she was caught, but they suddenly cleared and they were faced with a cleft in the mountainside which was hidden from outside view by the trees and bushes. Under the cleft was a small clearing where the black dragon waited, his red eyes burning brightly in the semi darkness.

Georgina quickly took in her surroundings looking for any possible means of escape, but with the two guards and Felspar so close to her, the whole idea appeared to be hopeless. The only way out seemed to be four small tunnels inside the back of the cleft.

"Move over there!" said the black dragon as he ushered her towards the cave entrance.

Georgina stumbled and steadied herself with her hand on a large rock. For some reason her mind had taken time to register what it already knew about her unfamiliar surroundings. When the hood had been taken off of her earlier she had seen the outline of what looked like a very long wall snaking its way along the top of the big hills in the distance. Occasionally it had been broken by a small tower and despite not having much of a liking for geography at school, she felt sure she must be in China as it had looked like a part of the Great Wall.

"Why have you brought me to China?" asked Georgina, mentally trying to work out how long she had been captive and surely someone would have alerted her father and the SSDP.

The two guards exchanged worried glances and for a split second Meredith looked stunned but she quickly regained her composure.

"Well now, we are a clever girl aren't we? You see Felspar I told you she was the right one for this task!" replied Meredith haughtily.

"Then let her get on with it then!" growled the dragon as he pushed Georgina towards the yawning caves. Georgina had no idea what was expected of her and resisted, digging in her heels.

"None of that, you silly girl... It's really quite simple...you just have to go down one of these little tunnels and collect an object for me... after that, I will set you free" explained Meredith patiently, tapping her nails on the rock face.

"What object?" asked Georgina, mistrusting her captor.

"Just a little something which I want you to fetch for me... that's all" Meredith cajoled.

"And what if I don't?" resisted Georgina with more bravery than she felt at that moment.

"I would rethink that if I were you Miss Penfold... you see we need you for the job because you are small enough to fit down that hole" replied Meredith in a cold voice, "we would have used Angus Munro but he was a bit big for some of the tunnels below and we decide to obtain your services instead!"

"You have Angus as well... where?" shouted Georgina frantically looking around for her best friend.

"Yes we have your beloved Angus and if you don't do as I say you'll never see your precious little hero again!" mocked Meredith nastily.

At that news, the young protector's heart fell and Felspar shoved her towards the first of the tunnels. She really did not have a choice now that she knew Angus would not be on his way to save her.

Georgina studied the four tunnels and none of them looked very inviting. One more shove from the black dragon and she was near the first of the tunnels. They were extremely narrow and barely big enough for her to squeeze into. In fact she was beginning to doubt she would fit in and she tried to stall.

"Can I at least have a torch?" she asked turning to Meredith.

The former SSDP member patted her pockets theatrically looking for a torch.

"I'm sure I had it here somewhere..." she replied, then suddenly stopping to look at Georgina, "Oh I'm sorry my dear... I seem to have forgotten it!"

The two men behind Meredith chuckled at the joke as Felspar and Meredith grinned maliciously at their hapless captive's expense.

"Enough stalling!" growled Felspar as he nudged her again.

Georgina turned to face her fate and it was dark, cold and lonely. As she peered into the tunnels the first two appeared to drop rapidly downwards and she did not fancy placing her body into them. The third looked more promising but no more inviting and the fourth's inside was wet and covered in green slime.

"Take great care of the object won't you... it's very important to us!" Felspar sneered.

It was the black dragon's parting shot and as laughter echoed around the cleft, Georgina felt more helpless than she had ever done before. She looked down and saw her laces were untied. She bent down to retie the laces of her walking boots, giving herself time to think and reassess the situation. 'What would Angus do?' she thought, mentally pulling herself together. Here she was alone and scared in a very unpleasant situation in a remote part of China. She didn't appear to have much choice and although still scared she fingered her dragon brooch as a talisman to reassure herself.

Chapter 11

'Action or Inaction, That is the Question'

"Now Angus let's not start jumping to conclusion, for all we know Meredith might have had nothing to do with any of this" replied Rathlin, who knew all too well how determined the lad could be once he got an idea in his head.

"But it makes sense Rathlin... who else would do this?" argued Angus.

"Granted, no-one we know of... but Meredith is not the only bad person around and we have no evidence" countered Rathlin.

"I think we should start looking in the countries where she has business interests..." Angus tailed off as he sensed the disapproval coming long distance down the phone.

The Tek's had a problem as they felt a certain responsibility, almost parental, for the boy and yet they knew him well enough to trust his hunches; even when this was outweighed by their own common sense. They were also deeply concerned about Georgina's disappearance and had no better suggestion.

"Okay Angus let's do this. We will check our sources to see where Meredith is and you stay put until we get back to you... Deal?" replied Rathlin after the pause.

"I guess I can stay here for now, but as soon as you know, please call me!" replied Angus reluctantly.

Angus went back outside to tell Pyrra the news and he replayed the conversation and the agreement that he was not to go back to Calmor just yet and wait to see if Meredith was still on British soil or not.

They were to return to the UK as planned tomorrow and Pyrra could see that Angus was not happy with this inaction. Angus sat on the steps of the large villa, his head hung in despair.

"I am sorry my friend. Georgina is special to you and it is hard to sit here and not be able to do anything, even though that woman might have a business in this region" said Kadin in an attempt to console his fellow dragon protector.

Suddenly Angus looked up at Kadin and smiled.

"Kadin, you're a genius!" he said and he jumped up, spun around and ran back inside the villa.

Kadin looked at Pyrra, a look of total surprise on his face.

"Oh no!" she said, "You had better go and see what he is up to."

As Kadin followed Angus up the stairs Wymarc smiled at Pyrra for the first time since his arrival. 'Perhaps now we will get somewhere' he said.

Upstairs in Kadin's room, Angus busily typed on the computer. He had just completed his first search when Kadin entered.

"Angus, what are you looking for?" asked Kadin.

"I am checking for a list of Meredith's businesses worldwide... now if I can just refine this a little more... yes, here it is!" said Angus triumphantly.

"Here is what?" asked a confused Kadin,

"Meredith has a list of her companies on her parent website which I needed to find and this will tell us where the nearest of her worldwide offices is..." replied Angus hitting the print key, "and then we can go visit them!"

"But we were told to stay here... in Dubai, were we not?"

"No, we were told to stay in Dubai... and anyway they won't know, so we can at least rule them out now to save a bit of time later" answered Angus, "and anyway, it was your idea!"

Angus grabbed the printout and ran back downstairs, leaving a slightly flustered Kadin standing by the desk. The immaculately dressed Arab boy thought, 'This must be how

Georgina feels when she participates in one of Angus' adventures'. A little scared, but also excited, he followed after his headstrong friend.

By the time he caught up with Angus the protector was already explaining his plan to Pyrra and the she did not look convinced.

".... and it looks like India is the closest office from here and I think we can get there in a couple of hours" finished Angus.

"Now Angus what were you told by Rathlin, you know he would not approve of this!" replied Pyrra.

"Come on Pyrra, the lad's right, we just can't sit here and do nothing. At least this is productive and what's the worst thing that can happen?" said Wymarc, supporting Angus.

Pyrra looked at Wymarc, Angus, Nehebkau and then Kadin. All of them appeared to be on her young protector's side and she knew it was an argument she would never win.

"Perhaps we can go home by way of India to check out one of Meredith's companies as it is kind of on the way" added Wymarc imploringly.

Pyrra was reluctant to deviate from the Tek's instructions and she knew the flight path was nowhere near India, but it did make sense to at least rule out the possibility of one location. She nodded her agreement.

"We are coming too as we are keen to help in the search for Georgina" added Kadin as he volunteered to accompany them.

The ski park and desert camp would have to wait for another visit to Dubai. Angus, concerned for his missing friend had other things on his mind now.

Chapter 12

'The Crushing Dark'

"Come on girly, we don't have all day!" Felspar jeered as he pushed her even closer to the first tunnel.

What a choice she had! None of the four holes looked particularly welcoming and all were narrow and dark. He shoved her again and this time she stumbled and fell over. She lay flat on the ground and inched her way towards the nearest of the tunnels.

"If you don't hurry up I will be forced to eat you and teenage bones tend to stick in my teeth so I would rather you just accepted your fate and got on with it!" growled Felspar from above her.

Georgina crawled forward on her hands and knees until her head was inside the nearest hole. It yawned into blackness and the smell that rose to meet her was horrendous. She crawled to the second and it was even steeper. The third did appear to be better however she went to the last to see if her first impression was accurate. As she bent to look, watery slime dripped from the above and ran down the inside of the tunnel. The only thing going for it was that it appeared less steep than the others. After some more thought she turned to give one last defiant scowl to her captors then Georgina took a deep breath and tipped herself head first into the third tunnel.

The tunnel was barely big enough for her to squeeze through and she wriggled her way forward and down. At first she tried to move forward on her stomach but it was too painful and slow. Then she managed to spin onto her back and move faster by using her arms to guide her with her hands on the ceiling and her back on the floor. Now she could use her legs more to push her body through the narrow tunnel. As she got more accustomed to the position her progress became faster and soon she did not notice the darkness as she was too busy concentrating on her movements. As she progressed the walls and floor of the tunnel became slimy and soon there was a horrible smell. She could not recognise the odour but it was like something very old and very nasty. Her focus wavered and her mind began to focus on the crushing darkness again. Georgina's heart began to beat harder and faster as her panic rose and she closed her eyes, concentrating on the next movement and inched her way forward, slowly. The protector breathed through her mouth so as not to be overcome by the stench in the tunnel. With her eyes closed, Georgina's other senses were heightened again and she at least had something to thank her captors for, having been deprived of her eyesight for several hours. She heard something and stopped. Georgina listened very carefully, focusing on what she was sure was breathing ahead of her in the tunnel. 'But what was it? Or was it just her imagination?' she wondered.

After about fifteen minutes of sliding on her back Georgina noticed that her body was moving faster along the floor of the tunnel and this was due to still more slime lubricating the walls. The tunnel began to drop downwards and she momentarily opened her eyes, but it was still as black as night and she could not see anything at all, not even her hand in front of her face. She closed her eyes tight and slowly struggled forward into the unknown. The tunnel continued to steepen and then suddenly she was stuck! It was so narrow her arms were pinned and her knees could not be raised more than a few inches. Again panic rose within the girl and she envisioned her body stuck forever thousands of miles from home and no one aware of where her rotting corpse lay. These dark thoughts threatened to overwhelm her and Georgina wrestled with her fears and with the confined space. She thrashed her body frantically in an effort to dislodge it but no matter how hard she tried she could not make any headway. She tried to go back but it was impossible with the slope now and she began to weep as despair took over. She had all but given up when her heel caught an edge of rock she did not feel before. As she carefully stroked her right foot slowly up and down Georgina hoped it was not her imagination. If only she could... yes! There it was. Georgina placed her hopes and her weight on that one edge of rock and pushed.

"Thank you!" she cried to the darkness as her body moved a couple of inches.

Using the merest of footholds the protector inched her way down until she could free an arm. Then using another edge or rock she managed to pull herself another foot or so. Georgina had to wriggle through with one arm pinned at her side, but somehow the girl managed to squirm through the narrowest of gaps.

After another pause for breath she pushed on and the going appeared to get a little easier as the slime increased and the tunnel diameter enlarged. She pushed with her feet to gain speed and instantly regretted it as it appeared she no longer needed to do so. The tunnel sloped dramatically downwards and Georgina squealed as she slid down out of control. Desperately she tried to grasp at the tight walls around her, but the slippery surfaces would not allow her to grip. They say the strangest thoughts go through a person's mind when they are in danger and Georgina's was. 'Thank goodness I have gloves on or my hands would be ripped to shreds!' However her speed continued to increase and gathering momentum the young protector sped down the sloping tunnel, like a bullet in a gun barrel, as it became steeper and steeper. Georgina realised she was hurtling downward head first and would eventually hit the bottom. Frantically she started to scrabble at the sides of the tunnel!

Chapter 13

'Passage to India'

Three dragons and two protectors took to the skies above Dubai, but Angus was no longer in the mood for sightseeing. His mind was completely focused on finding Georgina and getting her back to safety. He knew in his heart of hearts that going to India was a long shot and that Rathlin was probably right about Meredith however that would mean that the dreams he was having were all a figment of his imagination and how would he tell anyone that another dragon was visiting him in his sleep to show him that Meredith was the culprit behind this latest mischief. Kadin sat on Nehebkau and had changed into clothing more suitable for a journey such as the one they were embarking on. Wymarc took the lead and they headed eastwards over the mountains that bordered the United Arab Emirates and Oman. Soon they were over the Indian Ocean leaving the Middle East behind them.

"Wymarc, I think your geography is not too good... India is definitely not on the way back home!" called Pyrra. Wymarc just smiled.

"It really depends on which way around the globe you travel" he replied.

Angus smiled and was glad to be doing something purposeful, although he was very worried about Georgina, especially if his assumption was correct and that crazy woman Meredith had taken her. He had the address in Mumbai where the Quinton-Jones office was located and if she was there he intended to confront her. His plan did not extend much beyond that.

As they flew across the Indian Ocean they reached a large continent and a sprawling city that appeared to cover the entire visible land mass. Wymarc descended in height and it was clear that this was their destination. As they neared the vast city Angus could see that it was built around a series of natural bays, the biggest of which was on the eastern side of the main centre. He was amazed at the multitude of boats around the cities shores and even more stunned at the amount of cars he saw in the roads. The traffic was so thick in every direction he looked that it was difficult to really see the road at all. The roads pulsed with cars, buses, trucks and motor cycles of every description and colour. He watched as motorcycles dodged and weaved between cars and trucks, and he was amazed that no one was injured as it appeared to be extremely disorganised. Wymarc looked for a suitable place to land and he spotted a busy park within the urban jungle of buildings. Following his lead they landed at the edge of the grass and it was decided that the humans would have to find their way to the office on foot. They left the dragons safe in their invisibility.

"We'll be back soon" said Angus to Pyrra.

"Don't worry, I will make sure they don't get into any trouble" replied Pyrra, "We will wait on the roof of that building and watch for your return.

The boys walked up a bustling side street unsure of which direction they should go. Kadin knew how to speak some Hindi and he asked the way to the offices. Fortunately the man they spoke to spoke English and he also knew the area they were looking for.

"You can travel there faster if you use one of the auto rickshaws over there" replied the gentleman.

Angus and Kadin thanked the man for his help and
decided to go with his recommendation. They walked up to
a line of small three wheeled taxis, all painted black with a
yellow stripe around the front window. They jumped into
the first rickshaw which had red seats and a black canopy
for a roof. Angus had never expected anything like this and
he wondered if it was safe. The driver understood the
instructions from Kadin and they were off; speeding
through the street and out into the main road, weaving
through the static cars and trucks all honking in their
frustration. Angus hung on tight to the bars at his side as
the driver appeared to be in a hurry. The three-wheeler did
not go very fast in comparison to a car, but the driver
weaved in and out of the traffic, all the time tooting the
rickshaws horn. In fact all the drivers tooted the horns of
the vehicles they drove and what had looked like a mess
from the air actually appeared to have a sort of flow as the
bikes, cars, buses and taxis danced around each other
albeit very slowly indeed. Angus looked at Kadin and he
appeared to be enjoying the journey.

"This is wonderful, don't you think?" asked the Arab
boy.

"Yes; if you have a death wish!" replied Angus smiling.

The driver continued to dodge through the traffic and at times Angus thought a motorcyclist was going to end up inside the rickshaw beside him, which would have been easy as the vehicle did not have any doors. He watched in amazement as the busy multi coloured buses went by, so full; they had people hanging out of the doors. However the most astonishing thing he saw was a man sitting on top of an elephant. Now this in itself was not unusual, but the fact that he was guiding the elephant down the busy road was! Angus turned to Kadin with a look of 'did you just see what I just saw' and both boys laughed at the wonder of it all. The driver brought them to a built up area and eventually to the office address. Kadin paid in dollars which the man appeared to be okay with and they quickly entered the building and looked at the list of company names on the wall inside. Angus checked his printout and the office was there on the third floor. They entered the lift and as they stood silently watching the numbers climb, Angus felt nervous as to what he might find. 'Did he really expect to walk in and find Georgina here?' he thought to himself; His instincts told him no, and he was sure the others thought he was being silly and naive, but he had to do something. The dreams he had were repeating the same event over and over. An event he had never experienced, but the strange thing was that the blue dragon did not say the same things every time. It was obviously a warning, but about what? In fact the dragon had tried to explain things, but Angus had still not understood them as they did not make any sense. A bell dinged snapping him from his internal dialogue and the lift doors opened. They quickly located the offices only to find that the front door was lying ajar. Angus pushed the door gently as if expecting someone to jump out on him, but when nothing happened he walked into a dull and dirty reception area. The lights were off and at first Angus thought it was because they had come on a Saturday.

"I do not think it is a good day to come if we want to meet someone" said Kadin.

"I don't think anyone will be here in the near future" replied Angus picking up a notice on the reception counter, flanked by discarded plastic water cups.
He read that the offices were closed due to market conditions and that all staff would be made redundant with immediate effect. Sure enough the offices appeared empty with no sign of activity. Just then a security guard popped his head in the door and said something that Angus did not understand. Kadin tried to answer him, but his Indian

vocabulary was not extensive enough to get the message across.

"Why are you doing here sir?" asked the man in broken English.

Kadin explained that they were looking for Meredith's company and the guard explained that the people moved out of the office some weeks ago and the company no longer traded from India.

"Can we look around a little please?" asked Kadin politely.

"Yes sir that will be not a problem sir" replied the man before leaving them.

Angus thought it was very nice of the guard not to chase them out of the building and they began to explore. It was clear that the employees had left in a hurry because paperwork lay scattered over the desks and floor. All the doors were unlocked and Angus searched the empty offices with Kadin to try and find something that would help them. What that was, Angus did not know, but perhaps they would find some clue that would help them. It became clear there was nothing left in the rooms except dead pot plants, paper cups and a few plans on the walls depicting various drilling rigs and vessels presumably owned by Meredith's company.

"I don't think we are going to find anything here my friend" said Kadin quietly.

"Yes, I know, I just..." began Angus before sticking on his words and causing Kadin to think his fellow protector was upset.

"It is difficult for you, I know, but perhaps the others have found something out, we are not the only ones searching" said Kadin reassuringly.

The real reason Angus had stopped talking was because of something he had seen on the desk nearest them. It was dated 6 weeks ago but it appeared to be a communiqué between this office and the Hong Kong office about one of the drilling rigs that Meredith owned. He picked it up and began to read aloud;

"Rig departure from Singapore on Monday with all modifications for CEO visit completed. ETA in Hong Kong between 8-10 days, weather permitting. Preparations for CEO arrival in Hong Kong ongoing" Angus looked at Kadin. "Now we at least know where Meredith is!"

"You realise how far away Hong Kong is don't you?" asked Kadin, pointing to a map of the world on a wall across the office.

Both boys went to look more closely and Angus could see that Hong Kong was much further to the East than he had imagined. He folded the piece of paper and put it in his pocket before they left rather dejectedly to head back and find the three dragons at the park. They flagged down another rickshaw and both boys sat quietly in the back, lost in their respective thoughts.

Ten minutes later they were back at the same spot that they had left the dragons and Angus was glad that Pyrra had taken refuge on a rooftop. The whole park was full of people of every age and the majority of them were playing cricket!

The young protector was stunned by the sight of literally thousands of men and boys playing cricket; so many in fact that it was hard to tell who was playing with whom.

"This is the most popular pastime in the whole of India. We have many Indians working in Dubai and they play there as well" said Kadin in explanation.

"I've played in school but I've never seen anything like this!" replied Angus, incredulously.

"I have never played and to be honest the whole thing looks very confusing" said Kadin.

As the dragons landed beside them Angus tried to explain the rules to the Arab boy and the dragons were totally bemused by the whole thing. The dragons soon lost interest as the rules were far too complicated and eventually Angus gave up. As they sat in silence enjoying the colourful scene, a boy a little bit younger than Angus approached them. The boy looked in awe, and the two protectors thought it was because they were from another country. Then Angus realised the boy was not just looking at Angus and Kadin, but beyond them. Worried, Angus glanced towards the dragons wondering if they had mistakenly forgotten to stay invisible. The boy hesitantly moved closer and sat down beside Angus, still looking up at the dragons. Shyly he turned to Angus and lent towards him, touched his sleeve and whispered in his ear.

"Where did you find so many dragons?"

Chapter 14

'The Seeker'

Georgina had visions of her body flying head first from the end of the tunnel and straight into a wall or rock. Or worse still the bottom of this tunnel would be a dead end. Either way, the result was the same and her rising panic had her scrabbling at the walls of the tunnel above her, desperate to find a hand hold or ridge to slow her descent. She started to sob with every failed attempt and she chastised herself for being so weak.

"Think... think... what would Angus do?" she said to herself.

The idea came to her in a flash and with all her strength she forced her arms and legs into the sides of the tunnel like an artificial tree being forced into a tube. Almost imperceptibly she slowed her plummet and encouraged by this she pushed against the sides as hard as she could; screaming painfully as she did. Her right glove slipped off her hand and she is forced to use her bare flesh on the slimy side of the tunnel; but slowly, Georgina managed to arrest her descent and the young protector eventually came to a stop.

Georgina lay on her back with her hands on her face and sobbed with relief. Now wedged fast in the slimy tunnel she waited in the dark with her eyes closed, tears trickling down her face. She concentrated on her heartbeat and tried to calm herself down a bit. Slowly, but surely, the rhythm reduced until at last she felt calm enough to continue. Her legs ached from their braking effort and the palm of her right hand was scraped and bleeding. She could feel the wetness of the slime sting the fine cuts and instinctively she lifted her hand from her face to look at the damage. Georgina opened her eyes and instead of complete darkness was amazed to discover she could see a faint light. At first this confused the girl and she looked down the tunnel hoping to discover the light source. But all she saw was darkness. It appeared to be very near her

 and then she realised where the light was coming from. Georgina looked down towards the precious brooch her father had given her when she became a dragon protector. The small piece of Dragonore set within the eye on the silver dragon brooch was glowing and providing just enough light to see

a short distance within the tunnel. Georgina's heart was instantly lifted and encouraged by this good fortune she eased her body further down the shaft.

Her progress was much more steady and cautious this time and within a few minutes the tunnel opened up into a bigger room. Her head and shoulders were no longer supported and she used the brooch to find out where the floor was; or if indeed there was a floor; suddenly she dropped from the high opening. Georgina managed to turn a little in mid air like, but not being a cat she did not land on her feet. She was lucky not to land on her face and used the light from the brooch to see what her options were realising she could almost stand up now. The smell in this part of the tunnel was much worse and she made a concerted effort to breathe through her mouth otherwise she would surely be sick. Although the light from the brooch gave her comfort in such a dark place she wished with all her heart that Meredith had at least been kind enough to give her a torch; although she probably would not have been able to hold it in the cramped conditions anyway.

"As if Meredith would think about making the ordeal more bearable!" she said.

Georgina thought she was crazy for talking to herself, but if it kept her sane, she did not care; Georgina really didn't like being squashed in small dark places. The girl looked around the small pothole section she was in and it was barely big enough to allow her to stand up. It did at least give her a respite from the claustrophobic conditions she had just been in and she was pleased to no longer be head first. Two more tunnels faced the one she had entered from, and as she looked at them Georgina had one to her left and one to her right. While she was deciding which one to take she moved forward slightly to inspect them more closely and looked at the floor when she discovered she was standing in a puddle.

"Oh great... more slimy water!" she said sarcastically. Then she noticed that her missing glove had slid down the tunnel behind her and she smiled as she bent to pick it up. A sudden noise made her spin around and she stood motionless, barely able to breathe. 'Did I really hear something?' she thought, and as she listened her heart beat louder in her chest. Slowly and quietly she put her glove back on and stepped forward towards the choice of tunnels. Both looked exactly the same and she bent her head forward to crawl into the right hand tunnel. A strange gurgling growl echoed from within and around the small cavern she stood in and she jumped back in fright. Georgina listened intently for a repeat of the sound and she was rewarded almost immediately as another growl emanated from one of the tunnels, but which, she was not sure.

"Felspar?" she muttered under her breath, "Is that you? This is creepy enough without you playing tricks!" No answer came back other than an eerie silence.

"That's all I need, that horrible dragon throwing his voice to scare me... well it's not working!" she called to the darkness, not very convincingly. The darkness called back in the form of another gurgling growl and she held her breath so as not to give her presence away. Georgina listened intently, and could hear that the noise was getting louder and whatever was making it was surely getting nearer. She realised with horror that it was not Felspar playing tricks on her and without another thought she hastily dove into the left hand tunnel and hoped she would not meet whatever it was that appeared to be seeking her out!

Chapter 15

'A Sticky Wicket'

As a hundred games of cricket played simultaneously Angus stared in shock at the young lad and then at the dragons behind him. It took him a few seconds to come up with an answer, and even then it was not that convincing.

"Dragon's, what dragons?" replied Angus, looking around theatrically and feeling a bit foolish at the same time.

The young boy looked at Angus, looked at the dragons behind them and then asked.

"You cannot see the three dragons behind you?" Kadin tested the young boy in Hindi.

"What dragons do you mean?"

The Indian boy just smiled and pointed at Pyrra who raised her eyebrows in a gesture that confirmed to Angus what he already knew; that they were still invisible, but somehow this young Indian lad could see them!

"If you can really see dragons, why are you not running away scared?" asked Angus.

"You are with them and they do not harm you; so why should they harm me?" replied the boy logically; "They don't usually eat people anyway" added the lad.

"This is not the first dragon you have met, is it?" asked Angus astutely.

"Indeed not... I have met one dragon before today, but she told me that she was the last of her kind... she will be so pleased to hear I have found more!" answered the boy excitedly.

"You must have some Dragonore, where did you find it?" asked Kadin.

"I am not sure what you mean... perhaps you mean the bluestone..." replied the boy as he pulled a dirty piece of rock from his shirt pocket.

"Yes, that is Dragonore and it allows humans to see hidden dragons" explained Kadin. "It is very rare and you are lucky to have found it; and a dragon!"

"Then I am very blessed indeed as I did not know this... You both must be an authority on dragons since you have three with you" said the boy.

"We don't own the dragons... we are protectors and they are our friends!" replied Angus with a smile.

"Clearly I have a lot to learn; please, will you teach me to become... a protector?" asked the boy fervently.

Angus looked at Kadin, who nodded.

"What's your name?" asked Angus.

"Tarak!" replied the young boy smartly.

"And what age are you Tarak?"

"10 years old... well nearly 11!"

"Where did you find your Dragonore?" asked Angus mimicking Rathlin's proper line of questioning and causing a snigger from Pyrra as she recognised his parody.

"In Agra; next to the Taj Mahal!" replied Tarak.

"The Taj Mahal... Tell me how you met the dragon?" The young boy paused for the first time and seemed to collect his thoughts.

"I found the strange stone last the summer in the gardens of the Taj Mahal. I placed the bluestone, sorry Dragonore, in the pocket of my kurta. I had stayed outside playing in the tranquil gardens whilst my parents visited the mausoleum. It started to get hot so I decided to go and find some shelter. On my way to the Mausoleum I saw a dragon strolling across the lawns and drinking from one of the water channels. I could not believe my eyes and I pinched myself" explained Tarak in a very animated way.

"And is that when you met the dragon?" asked Angus.

"Oh no" replied Tarak, "I was not sure if the dragon was friendly or not!"

"So what did you do then?" asked Kadin.

"The dragon started to head towards the Taj Mahal and I was brave and followed it to its hiding place within the mausoleum itself!" said the boy triumphantly.

"That was brave" said Angus honestly.
Tarak smiled at the praise and continued.

"I watched it morph into a marble inlay pattern running all the way round the inside of the walls... They look very much like dragon heads" continued the boy, "and I felt even braver having come this close to a dragon and decided to look closer at the exact spot where it had disappeared!"

"What happened?" asked Kadin.

"I got up really close to the pattern on the wall and that is when the dragon hissed at me and told me to go away!" The young boy sat up and looked expectantly at the two protectors; obviously finished with his story.

"So have you managed to speak to the dragon much since then?" asked Angus.

"I'm afraid not... after it told me to go away I thought it best to not aggravate it... but I do keep looking for it when I go there!" he added quickly.
The two protectors relaxed as they realised they had discovered a fellow protector quite by chance, even though he didn't know that he was one!

"Well Tarak, I have a lot to teach you, but first I had better tell you about what we do and introduce you to our friends behind us!" replied Angus smiling.

The newest dragon protector literally bounced up and down on the bench they were sitting on and some of the people nearby stared at his antics. Angus calmed him down with a gentle pat on the shoulder.

The dragons were introduced one by one and, as was there way, each of them politely welcomed Tarak to the ranks of the SSDP. Angus went on to explain all about the Secret Society of Dragon Protectors, how Calmor was the home of the SSDP and all about the hierarchy of dragon-kind. Tarak sat open mouthed during the whole conversation and when Angus told him about how many dragons they had found, he had to place his hand on the boys shoulder to calm him down again as he kept jumping up like a jack in the box. After giving a brief history of the last two years Angus went on to explain about the importance of Krubera, the Great Hibernation and the Cor Stan itself. By this time Tarak could barely sit still, such was his excitement; however when Angus told him about Ceamantya and Aedan the young Indian boy squealed with delight.

"Oh how I would love to see two baby dragons!" he shouted rather too loudly.

Pyrra and the others laughed, but Angus looked around at the people now staring and gave the boy a stern look.

"Now the main thing for you to remember is that you must keep all of this secret!" said Angus. "No-one can know and if you tell anyone, you will lose your Dragonore and your status as a protector!"

The young boy looked crestfallen.

"But... I promise. I won't tell anyone... Not even my sister!" he replied earnestly.

"As long as you remember all of what I have told you, it will be okay, but secrecy is the only way and I cannot help you become a protector if you cannot keep a secret!" said Angus.

"Please, please, please teach me Angus!" pleaded Tarak. "Can I become the protector of the dragon I found?"

"Well we will need to speak to the dragon and let it decide" replied Angus.

"But Agra is so far away and my family are here to visit my Auntie in Mumbai... they won't go back for days!"

"Then I guess we will need to fly there by dragon and now I will need to teach you something else about them" smiled Angus.

Again the young boy sat stunned as Angus explained about the powers of dragons and that they could fly to Agra in an hour.

They watched a little more cricket as Tarak went to get the rest of his things. Having decided to fly to Agra and see this new dragon for themselves; Angus felt somewhat comforted to be doing something useful for the SSDP. The whole time he had been speaking to Tarak his mind had never wandered far from Georgina's plight or the danger she might be in and even Angus could not have imagined the ordeal she had been put through.

Chapter 16

'Minotaur's Labyrinth'

Georgina forced her body on through the unpleasant tunnel. Fear drove her protesting muscles into action. The strange gurgling continued to echo down the tunnel from behind her. Whatever the thing was she was sure she did not want to meet it and with as much energy as she could muster, Georgina put as much distance as she could between herself and the noise in the tunnel. Her imagination worked overtime as she literally propelled her body head first through the tunnel. Strangely, images of a past history lesson entered into her mind and she struggled to grasp the thought as she fought her way downwards. Suddenly a moment of clarity descended and she could not see what her mind had been screaming out to her all along. Her mind's eye filled with images of a vast maze, designed to confuse and waylay adventurers from their quest. It was the Minotaur's labyrinth and in that network of wrong turns and dead ends the eventual outcome was... 'No! That's not going to happen to me' she thought in retaliation to the last image. At least now Georgina knew where she was; and it was inside a warren of tunnels designed for one purpose. To force anyone silly enough to come down here into the clutches of the beast that now apparently tracked her. Now that she could see, the young protector recognised tool marks on the tunnel walls and it was obvious that they had been constructed in this fashion to make it as difficult for any intruder as possible.

Doubling her efforts Georgina pushed onwards but then she realised that something had changed. She stopped and listened keenly for sounds of the monster... Nothing! 'Could it have given up?' she thought. Very carefully and quietly she moved forward. The tunnel was still cramped; however it was big enough now to move a little better than when she had been able to in the first tube. She put her hands forward to grip the tunnel below her and suddenly she fell forward as her hands met with air instead of rock. Off balance Georgina flailed desperately trying to gain a handhold, but it was too late and she fell forward into yawning darkness.

Chapter 17

'Agra's Secret'

Now airborne, the dragons carried their young riders up into the skies above Mumbai; the newest recruit squealing with delight. It was his first time on a dragon and the other protectors smiled at his enjoyment and recalled how they felt the first time they had flown with their dragons. The experience was thrilling to say the least and neither Kadin nor Angus would ever forget it. Pyrra led the three dragon's north and they stayed in formation with Wymarc looking after the excitable Tarak. After a few minutes they passed over three lakes in a row then over the mountains beyond. Pyrra swept up the mountainside skimming the many trees that grew on the slopes. Angus could hear Tarak laugh in delight as they swept over the crest and down the other side.

"You're showing off, aren't you?" said Angus leaning forward to tease her.

"No, of course not!" she replied with a grin.

As they picked up more speed they soon left the mountains behind, with a vast valley now stretched in front of them. Angus could see a massive river in the distance, its banks flanked by fields on either side. It was a clear day and he could see for miles in every direction.

"India is huge" he called to Pyrra, who nodded in agreement.

They continued due north over many plains and soon saw the sprawling city of Agra below them. Angus saw another sprawling city below and it appeared to stretch all the way to the horizon. As they flew lower he began to make out some features and then the ultimate jewel, the Taj Mahal itself. From this viewpoint the large river north of the city formed a 'u' shape into the heart of the area with the Taj Mahal hanging off the southern bank like a pendant on a blue necklace. The river undulated east and west in lazy loops for as far as he could see and they came down to land in a scrub area on the banks of the river.

More magnificent than he could ever have imagined the Taj Mahal grew in stature the nearer they got to it. Sunlight bounced off the white marble of the main building and Angus could see hundreds of people walking around the ancient wonder. Pyrra, Nehebkau and Wymarc looked for a suitable landing site and flew back over the long causeway and settled down in a relatively secluded area at the front to wait and see what the boys found. Tarak, so shy when he first approached Angus, now took on the role of tour guide. Unlike millions of visitors to the Taj Mahal whose first glimpse of the magnificent four hundred year old white marble Crown Palace was through a pink limestone archway; Angus and the others had the pleasure

of first seeing it from the air. When they did enter through the usual tourist route Angus was still so overawed by the sight that he felt goose bumps ripple along his arms. He looked at Kadin and knew the Arab lad felt the same. This was the most incredible snapshot, as if through a window, but no photographs could ever truly capture the breath taking splendour of seeing that view first hand. Tarak had seen it many times, living close by and was amused to see his companions jaws drop like all the other tourists.

"Whenever Mughal rulers built a tomb they also constructed a courtyard through which it could be entered, in this case the pink sandstone wall" explained Tarak as he led the way through to the peaceful gardens.

Obviously enjoying being able to explain the rich history, Tarak continued with his tour.

"The gardens were supposedly modelled to resemble Paradise in the Islamic tradition which is why it is full of Cypress trees" he added.

The visitors absorbed the beauty of the place as they followed the watercourse they had seen from the air right up to the entrance plinth of the Taj Mahal itself. Tarak was enjoying himself immensely and was justifiably proud of his heritage. For years visitors have been drawn from all over the world to see this monument, which was nearly four hundred years old.

"All this was built by the grieving Emperor Shah Jahan as a burial place for his much loved young wife Mumtaz who died giving birth to their fourteenth child" continued Tarak.

"Fourteen children?" asked Angus incredulously.

"Indeed Angus" replied Tarak.

"Wow..." then realising he had interrupted, "Sorry Tarak, please continue."

"I am not boring you both?" asked the young boy.

"Not at all... We are finding this very interesting" replied Kadin.

"Oh goody" replied Tarak, then gathering his thoughts he continued, "The monument took 20 years to build and it is reported to have taken a 22,000 strong workforce to complete the task..."

Angus had been back to the Middle Ages and had seen for himself how difficult it was to build things in the past. Looking at the splendour and complexity of the buildings in front of him, he could understand why it would have taken them so long to build it 400 years ago.

"...It was a colossal feat of construction. The grief stricken widower planned an identical but black mausoleum for himself on the opposite bank of the river so that the two reflections would join and reunite the pair for eternity."

"What happened to the black palace" asked Kadin.

"It was never built as the Shah was overthrown by one of his sons and was imprisoned for nine years before his own death; ironically in the monument he built" explained

Tarak pointing to the central piece of this architectural
wonder.

Reflecting on this for a moment the boys followed the
crowds up the marble steps, gazing about them as they
entered the building made from translucent white marble
brought by elephant from the region of Rajesthan. Tarak
was in full flow, enjoying his rapt audience.

"Although he adored his wife it seems the Shah was a
cruel Emperor who had killed his own brothers to ensure
he would rule the Mughal Empire..." he added.

Angus could imagine that things were very cut throat back
then and he had images of the Emperor's troops fighting
from the top of elephants attempting to defeat a rival army.

As Kadin wandered off with Tarak deep in conversation
Angus took a moment to look at the internal structure and
he was amazed that the building, so simplistic in its
symmetrical pattern on the outside, did not prepare you for
the rich decoration on the inside. He heard the young
Indian boy proudly announce that there were twenty eight
different types of precious and semi precious stones used
including lapis lazuli from Afghanistan; jasper from the
Punjab; jade and crystal from China; and turquoise from
Tibet... 'A perfect place to find a dragon' thought Angus as
he caught them up.

"Interestingly, the whole building is completely symmetrical and the only thing which spoils that symmetry is the cenotaph of Shah Jahan himself..." continued Tarak, who was turning out to be a veritable fountain of knowledge and authority on the great monument, "which was never in the plans and hastily added after his death when the projected black companion monument across the river was abandoned" said the lad finally taking a breath. Kadin looked about and seized his moment to ask an important question.

"I can't see anything dragon shaped in here? How can a dragon be hiding in this place?" he enquired.

"I am not sure about the dragon shapes but that is where the dragon hides" replied Tarak pointing up on the wall.

Angus looked at the wall that Tarak was pointing to and could see not just one, but a whole row of dragon heads. They were disguised as swathes of flowers in the rich marble inlay, running right around the room. He smiled at the cleverness of the hiding place, as you had to really look to see dragon shapes. He would need to explain the dragon themed object rule to Tarak before he left.

"Which one is it?" he asked Tarak, but the boy did not need to answer.

Since they all had Dragonore they could detect the location of a hidden dragon and all three pieces of Dragonore were glowing fiercely. With so much of the precious stone in close proximity the hidden dragon could not deny their existence any longer and without any further warning a golden Asian dragon morphed out from the wall decoration and stood in front of them.

The beautiful creature's appearance filled the empty room and blinded them in its magnificence. Almost immediately Angus noticed that this splendid creature looked to be the same kind of dragon as Nehebkau. This meant that he was not the last Asian dragon after all and with the head bereft of spikes and the body smaller in size, he had already worked out that this was a female.

"Get away from here or I'll eat you!" said the dragon unconvincingly.

"No you won't!" replied Angus, "and we are members of the Secret Society of Dragon Protectors"

"They have been disbanded for a long, long time, so you surely do not expect me to believe that; do you?" said the dragon, "Who are you and what do you want?"
Angus recalled Pyrra telling him that dragons in hiding did not like to be discovered and this could make them initially prickly towards any approach. The secret to overcoming

this was to be courteous and proper introductions were important.

"I am sorry for the intrusion madam; we are from the SSDP and my name is Angus" he replied calmly.
Kadin had never heard Angus speak so politely and the Arab boy stared in shock at his friends display.

"This is Kadin another protector from Dubai, and this young man is Tarak; whom I think you met before" continued Angus.
The dragon was now firmly focused on him, and as she was still not saying anything, the young protector gave a polite bow.

"We are very pleased to meet you" he added and this appeared to delight the dragon and finally break the ice.

"Well it is certainly good to see a human with manners!" she replied. "I am Min-Li and I have lived here for close to 300 years and you are the first human I've met that knows how to conduct himself properly in the face of a dragon. You could teach that young man something as all he did was run away!"
She was referring to Tarak and the young Indian boy blushed when he realised he was being singled out.

"We are here on SSDP business and I would like you to meet the other dragons that accompanied us here" said Angus officiously.

"Well now that would be interesting... lead the way young sir!" replied Min-Li, looking distinctly more interested.

Now that the greetings were exchanged they went back outside into the sunshine and Angus explained about the work of the SSDP and how they were monitoring the number of dragons still alive and coming out of Hibernation. The boys discovered that Min-Li meant 'quick-witted' and that she too awakened from Hibernation when she heard Barfoot's message, but could not remember where the Cor Stan was located. Min-Li confirmed that she had only just met Tarak quite recently and although surrounded by many people on a daily basis, she was amazed to find one small boy who could actually see her.

"Tarak is one of our newest members and I am training him to be a protector" explained Angus, "If it was not for him we would never had found you and he is a quick learner!"

Tarak smiled shyly as the golden dragon eyed him cautiously.

"I suppose you will want him to be my protector?" she asked.

"Only if it pleases you... Of course I have been training him but with your help he will make a wonderful protector!" answered Angus smoothly.

The dragon seemed to ponder this proposition for a second or two before replying.

"Well I think I could knock him into shape and if you vouch for him I think he will suffice" said Min-Li.

This was all the excitement Tarak could take and he ran up to the dragon and wrapped his arms around her chest.

"Oh thank you Min-Li; you have made me so happy and I will be the best protector ever!" he said with his face pressed against her scales.

Kadin and Angus laughed, but realising they were drawing attention to themselves they calmed the young boy down. Angus was a little worried the affectionate display might have put the dragon off, but it appeared to have had the opposite effect as she appeared to have warmed to the young boy.

Kadin was overjoyed at the significance of this new discovery and couldn't wait to introduce Nehebkau to this stunning female. They led Min-Li, beyond the boundaries of the garden and the three other dragons performed the formal introductions, dragon style. He had seen it before but it was still good to watch and he quietly explained to Tarak what was happening. The dragon's introduced themselves, starting with the females and each bowed and gave their name. It was just like humans used to do many hundreds of years ago, but with much more formality and on a much larger scale.

"What are they saying?" asked Tarak.

"I don't exactly know as they are speaking in dragon" replied Angus, but then as he listened more intently he realised he could make out and understand some of the dragon's language.

This was strange and he began to listen more intently, shutting his eyes to concentrate.

"Are you okay?" asked Kadin, bringing Angus out of his trance.

Angus shook his head and nodded he was okay and the dragons, finished with the formalities began to speak in English once again. They discussed the many changes in the SSDP and Pyrra explained Angus' role in all of it, and now it was his turn to blush. Tarak now stared at Angus with a mixture of reverence and awe as he heard the many adventures he and Pyrra had been on. Soon the conversation moved on to the plight of all dragons and the dwindling numbers.

"So many of us have disappeared now... I have lost count of the numbers" said Pyrra sadly.

"You are the first Asian dragon we have found since Nehebkau" added Wymarc.

Nehebkau had not said much at all and all he had done was look at Min-Li since the introductions, but now he spoke.

"I thought I was alone in this world and the last of my kind" he said suddenly.

"We are not the last, but I chose not to go with the others and stay within" she explained.

"Within?" asked Angus now very interested in the conversation.

"Within refers to this world and that I chose to stay within it" she replied, "The others went to the Realm Beyond."

"Another realm... is that possible?" asked Kadin curiously.

"Yes it is and disenchanted with this world the Asian dragons found another world, a world beyond this one." Angus could barely believe it himself, but if someone had told him two years ago that he would meet a dragon that could stay invisible to all humans; use powers to speed up and slow down time; allow him to walk through fire unharmed; link with his mind and travel through time: he would have called them crazy. Considering all of that and more had in fact happened to him; he was convinced that this Realm Beyond actually did exist.

Soon Min-Li had explained that the realm was hidden in China and only one person knew of the location.

"The protector was chosen due to his ability to harness dragon powers, but that was over 2000 years ago and I am sure the knowledge is now lost" she added sadly.

"Can you remember the location of the other realm?" asked Nehebkau eagerly.

"I was never shown where it was exactly" replied Min-Li and she shook her head sadly.

A solemn silence descended on the group and Angus felt sorry for Nehebkau. He realised how much it meant to the dragon that there were others and now it looked as though he never would find them.

"Well at least I have found you!" said Nehebkau smiling.

Nehebkau and Min-Li discussed the demise of their species and shared stories. It appeared to Angus that they were getting on well and he strolled aimlessly along the wall wondering if he would ever find Georgina.

"Are you alright Angus?" asked Pyrra behind him having sensed his sadness.

"Yeah... I'm fine... just thinking about Georgina, that's all" he replied dejectedly.

"I never got to ask, but I assume you found nothing at the office?" she enquired.

"The company was shut down and no one works there anymore!" replied Angus.

"It is a pity that you did not find any sign of Meredith; I know you had pinned your hopes on..." added the green dragon, but before she had finished Angus was struggling to get something from his denim trouser pocket. He produced the paper he had lifted from the office and began to open it.

"I found this communication from one of her other offices and it explains that she was going to arrive in Hong Kong a couple of weeks ago!" he explained.

Pyrra just looked at him blankly, but she knew him too well and she waited on what he had to say next.

He then reached into his rucksack and pulled out a pocket sized world map.

"Do you realise that India is not too far from Meredith's Hong Kong office and it would be worth checking it out in case she has taken Georgina there?"

"I had a feeling you were going to suggest that!" she replied shrewdly. "I think you'll find it is a bit further away than you think!"

Angus had to agree that it was quite far and that would probably mean he would not make it home as planned, but he could not be this close and not try. Wymarc joined them with Kadin and he explained the proposal to them. Kadin agreed immediately and had secretly hoped that Angus would try something like this. The Arab boy knew the reputation Angus had and he felt they were on the cusp of another adventure.

"I think we should go" replied the blue dragon.

All eyes were fixed on Pyrra and not for the first time she looked into the eyes of her young protector. She knew how important Georgina was to him and she could not deny that she too wanted to find the girl more than anything else.

"We had better make tracks then if we are to get there tonight; but you will call your parents first and let them know you will be late getting home!" said Pyrra at last.

Her companions smiled at this wisdom and began to make preparations to leave.

The time spent in India had been very rewarding and they had found another dragon, but even though the discovery of Min-Li was extremely important it was taking them no nearer on their quest to find Georgina. Min-Li promised to return Tarak to his family in Mumbai and the young lad eagerly climbed on her back, excited about the second dragon ride in his young life. Now he had a dragon all of his own to protect and he waved goodbye to his new friends, pleased with his role as tour guide and dragon protector. The young Indian boy could not wait to see Krubera and Calmor; and the thought of meeting so many dragons left him almost speechless with excitement. The group took off one by one and it was a little reluctantly that Nehebkau left his new dragon friend and flew off towards the Far East.

Chapter 18

'Dinner is Served'

Georgina muffled a scream as she instinctively tucked her body, head protected, and rolled through the air. She had no idea how far she would fall, but fortunately she did not have time to ponder that as her shoulder blade made sharp contact with the rock below. The pain caused her to whimper slightly and her mind raced as she lay on her back listening intently for a sign her pursuer had resumed the hunt. The only thing she could hear was the dripping of water from the ceiling. No gurgling or growling emanated from the tunnels and she let out a long, quiet breath. She had not realised that she had held her breath and her heart pounded in her ears as the oxygen filled her body again. Gingerly, she sat up and rubbed the protesting shoulder while she tried to inspect her surroundings. The tunnel she had fallen from was about five feet above her head and fortunately for her the drop had not been that much. It was also providence that the floor was not jagged or she would be surely nursing more than a sore shoulder. After a few last rubs she stood up and looked at her new options. Hopefully the beast had lost her scent now and she would not be bothered by it anymore, but the sensible part of her brain told her that this was just a respite and she had better be on her toes. This time she could only see one exit and it appeared she had no choice but to go forward; realising that whatever hunted her would also only have one choice to make. 'Now if I only had a weapon' she thought and she began to look around the floor for anything that would suffice. Georgina looked all around the chamber and instinctively edged back towards the walls. She stood on a rock and did not notice it was wet. Her footing slipped, slapping her foot into a puddle. The splash echoed around the chamber, amplified by the shape of the small space. The young protector held her breath again as she listened intently. A screech emanated down the tunnel above her and without a moment's pause she raced across the chamber and dove into the only escape route she had.

Like a rat in a sewer she scurried along the tunnel as fast as she could. A few seconds later she popped out into another chamber similar to the one she was in before, but this time it had three more tunnels branching off it. Noises of pursuit emitted from the tunnel behind her and she knew she did not have much time to dally. 'I don't like this game!' she thought and she sprang into the right hand tube. By the sound of it the beast had just rolled into the chamber as she could hear it thrashing about. She had obviously just left in time and knew she needed to put more distance between her and whatever hunted her. Fear drove her onwards and all other thoughts were driven from her mind. Only a primal urge to survive existed now and when Georgina heard the growling noise coming down the tunnel behind her, she slithered down as fast as she possibly could, wondering where all this was going to end.

Not caring if the monster heard her or not, Georgina pushed her muscles harder. She would be okay just as long as she could keep ahead. This tunnel was longer than the last two and it seemed like ages before she fell out of the tunnel and into yet another small chamber. This time she landed on rags and at first she was confused as she extricated herself from the wet cloth. Georgina had grown used to the smell that had caused her nostrils such discomfort before, but in this chamber the stench was overpowering. When she looked down she noticed something white on the floor and she bent forward to get a better look in the dim blue light from her brooch. Instinctively her hand reached forward and turned the object over; immediately dropping it to the floor with a clatter.

"No! Please tell me I'm not in the beast's lair!" she said to herself quietly.

The young protector knelt to scan the floor and saw more bones. She had entered the dining room and she was surely the main course!

Chapter 19

'Phone Home'

Angus and Pyrra led the party eastwards and followed the Yamuna River for a time. Angus watched it curl and curve lazily across the landscape below. They continued on this path and the sun soon began to disappear behind them. Below he could see that it was becoming more mountainous and felt colder. Luckily he had brought some warmer clothes with him and as he pulled his jacket on he could see that Kadin was doing the same. He forced his arm into the other flapping sleeve and zipped it up. The protector had no idea where they were now, but on his left were snow capped mountains higher than any he had seen before. Angus had seen many mountains, but he could never have imagined anything like this. They went on forever. To his right was land as far as he could see and Pyrra continued her easterly flight path over and between the smaller peaks and the foot of the vast range they now followed. The lad soon gave in to sleep as the night sky erupted with stars and Pyrra left the vast mountain ranges of central Asia behind them, with a tired but determined Wymarc, close following behind.

Turbulence affects planes but it also affects all flying objects and it was the buffeting that woke Angus from his sleep. Kadin and Nehebkau kept in close behind as they made their way over a mountain side, densely covered in trees.

"Where are we?" called Angus to Pyrra.

"Somewhere in the north of Burma... I think!" she replied. "Welcome back!"

"Was I sleeping for long?" he asked, feeling rather guilty that he could sleep while she had to fly.

"About an hour... but don't worry, you should sleep while you can!" she called back smiling.

"Are you okay?"

"Of course... but I demand two extra sweets when we land!" she replied looking round at him.

Angus smiled and nodded his head in agreement patting his pocket. They continued along a vast valley with mountains on both sides covered in trees. Angus had never really seen jungle and the smell of the dense vegetation reached them even though they were high above the tree line. He looked at Kadin and the Arab lad appeared to be sleeping and Angus decided to take Pyrra's advice and he lay forward again; his face resting on her warm neck. With his eyes closed he listened to the rhythmic flapping of her wings. Surprisingly he could hear the noises of nocturnal creatures calling to each other in the jungle below and he drifted off to sleep again with their song in his ears.

The blue dragon appeared before him and smiled at Angus. The protector knew where this dream was going but he looked at the dragon as a sort of companion now. They had made the same journey in his dreams so many times now that Angus had almost begun to think of him as a friend. Except that a friend would not put you through the same harrowing ordeal every time you slept.

"Do we have to do this again?" asked Angus.

"I am sorry Angus but it is essential you are prepared" replied the blue dragon.

"Prepared for what?" asked Angus angrily. "All I do is wake up at the same point every time! What am I supposed to learn from this?"

"I cannot tell you any more than I already have... Just be patient... the time is coming soon and all will be revealed" replied the dragon mysteriously.

"I don't even know what that means! Can't you even tell me your name?" probed the lad desperately.

"My name is not important... only your task, and now it is time to travel there once more" replied the dragon.

Resigned to his fate Angus jumped up onto the back of the blue dragon and his immediate surroundings blurred.

The night wore on and the three dragons pushed ever eastwards towards Hong Kong. Soon they could see the bright city shining in the distance and with fresh vigour they sped forward for the last leg of their long journey. Pyrra was tired and what she longed for more than anything was a nice sleep and a cool bath. She hoped she would find both in Hong Kong. Suddenly Angus awoke with a shout.

"Are you okay?" she asked.

"Uh... yeah... yes I am" he replied drowsily.

"You were having that dream again, weren't you?" asked the dragon.

Angus was slightly stunned by the question as he had not told Pyrra anything about the dreams. In fact he had not told anyone and now that she had asked about them he knew the time was right to tell her.

"How do you know about the dreams?" he asked.

"I have heard you talk in your sleep during our journeys and you seem to be troubled by the same thing. What do I do to make you shout out my name like that?"

The image of Pyrra, claw raised above her head flashed into his mind. How could he tell her that his dream ends with her slashing at him with a fatal blow!

"It's complicated, but I keep seeing the same thing happen over and over and..." Angus explained but then could go no further.

"You do know that I would never hurt you Angus... We are bonded together in a friendship that can overcome every adversity" she said, turning her head to look at him. As he stared into her green eyes he knew in his heart that this was true. His dreams were just a figment of his over fertile imagination and he shook his head and smiled at her.

"You're right and it was just a stupid dream" he replied. The dragon seemed to consider his last comment before she turned to face the line of flight again.

"We are almost there" said Pyrra as she pointed in the direction of the sunrise.

Below them was an airport which had been built on what Angus assumed was reclaimed land. Pyrra instinctively followed a large multi-lane highway from the airport and Angus was amazed to see it crossed the gap between the islands using the longest bridge he had ever seen. The three dragons flew high above the early morning traffic and watched as the bridge reached a small island where the cars disappeared into a tunnel. The tunnel opened out the other side of the island onto another road bridge and from

there they were into a large harbour area. Everywhere
Angus looked in the harbour he saw boats of all shapes
and sizes. Clearly Hong Kong was a busy port and he
motioned for Pyrra to fly closer to Nehebkau.

"Where do you think the offices will be?" he shouted to
Kadin.

"Probably the Central Business District as that is where
my father always goes to when he visits Hong Kong"
replied the Arab lad. "Over there looks promising!"
Kadin had pointed across the watery expanse to the larger
island and as the early morning sunlight reflected off the

glass they saw a multitude of towers which appeared to be flowing down from the mountainside towards the harbour.

The travellers were absolutely exhausted and as soon as they landed they set about finding a place to stay as they had travelled all through the night. The boys managed to exchange some dollars and pounds which was all the currency they had between them, and found lodgings in a cheap and very small tourist hotel close to the business district. The three dragons went off to sleep in a park, and luckily the Asian climate made it quite pleasant to be outdoors at this time of year. Although it was now early on Sunday morning the two lads needed sleep and they trudged up to their room to get a few hours rest. Kadin reminded Angus that he still needed to call his parents and let them know he was going to stay longer. Angus thought about his mum and dad and the fact that they thought he was in Calmor. He really did hate having to lie to them and he resolved to tell them all when he got back. At least he would once he had Rathlin's permission and Pyrra's help. He pulled his mobile from his backpack and switched it on only to find he could not get a signal.

"Here, use mine" said Kadin as he threw his mobile across from his bed.

Angus thanked him and dialled the number for home. His mum answered in her usual posh phone voice and Angus explained that he would stay on another day at Calmor as the weather was bad and they could not get a boat.

"That's okay Angus, but don't you get into any boat until the weather calms down; you hear!" she replied, "Anyway I think your school is still shut as the weather has worsened here too."

"I won't Mum and don't worry about me, I'm fine" he replied. "Need to go... Love you... Bye!"

He ended the call and tossed it over to Kadin.

"Thanks mate!"

"You are most welcome, my friend" replied the Arab boy sleepily, having already text his father.

Kadin turned over and lay down to sleep, but Angus was overtired and had too many thoughts flitting through his mind. It took ages to get off to sleep in the compact twin bedded room he now shared with Kadin and when he eventually dropped off to sleep the dark blue dragon appeared again.

"Not again! We just did this" said Angus angrily.

"I can understand your frustration Angus but this time I have something else to show you" replied the dragon calmly.

Reluctantly Angus climbed on the dragon's back and the blurring started around him as before; however unlike the previous occasions they did not end up in the large room with everyone watching him. This time he found himself in what appeared to be an old prison cell. As the blurred floor and walls came into focus he could see someone lying on the floor and it took him a few seconds to realise that it was Georgina.

"Why are you showing me this? Where is she? If you know, please, tell me!" pleaded Angus.

"I cannot interfere more than I have Draca Gast and your destiny awaits you. I can only hope to guide you, but know that you are drawing ever nearer to her and you should trust your instincts..." the dragon faded along with those last words and Angus awoke with a start.

Now he knew that Georgina really was being held prisoner and that he was getting nearer to her. He wished the blue dragon had told him more but it was more than enough to drive Angus into action. He needed to find Meredith's company offices today and try to find out where she might be as he was sure that was the key to finding Georgina. After all he had been told to follow his instincts and that's exactly what he was going to do. But first he was going to follow his gut and it was telling him it was time to eat.

After waking Kadin both boys went down to the main street having showered and dressed in record time. The streets around the hotel were filled with a colourful array of shops selling everything from food to electronics. Street advertising signs filled every space conceivable the place was alive with noise and they quickly found a small cafe and discussed the next move.

"I think... we should be able to get directions... from the concierge... in the hotel" suggested Kadin in between mouthfuls of chocolate croissant.

This turned out to be the perfect plan as the concierge not only spoke very good English, but he also gave them a map and found them a taxi. Ten minutes later they arrived at the offices and Angus was taken aback by the height of the buildings and the amount of glass they had. The entire street was lined with glass towers and he could only imagine how many windows there were. The office building they wanted was open and this was a surprise to Angus as it was Sunday and he had expected it to be closed. They entered the tall office block and quickly located the correct floor. Angus hoped that Meredith had not shut down this office, but he had no need to worry as they found the offices thriving and busy. This was a stark contrast to the disappointment of the closed office in India. Angus took the lead and began to explain the situation to the neatly dressed woman on the reception desk.

"Excuse me; can we speak to Ms. Quinton-Jones please; it's a matter of great importance!" he said.

"I'm sorry but she is not in the office at present, can I take a message?" replied the woman.

"I wish you could, but this is something only she would want to hear and the message is very personal to her" replied Angus seriously.

"I... really can't help you..." said the young lady as she looked along the corridor, "You see, she is out of town and we don't know when she'll be back!"

Angus looked at the receptionist and could see that she was scared to tell them much more, but he thought of something that might just swing it for him.

"I understand..." he said as he turned to leave, "She will be disappointed though as it was about her hobby!"

The Asian receptionist had met the scary boss lady and guessed by Angus's demeanour that he was probably telling the truth. She had found her employer to be very strange and secretive and the rumours about her strange episodes in the UK were regular tea room gossip.

"Wait please!" called the receptionist just as Angus reached the lift doors.

"As I told you she is not in the country at present and is away on business... it is really bad luck as you only just missed her by a few days" explained the receptionist.

The lads looked crestfallen and the lady decided that it would surely do no harm to tell them more. Normally she would not give out such information but she could not see the harm in telling such polite young men and they could hardly follow her.

"She has gone off to one of the jack-up rigs in the East China Sea just off the coast of Shanghai" she added smiling.

The lads thanked her for her help and said they would be back when she returned from China. They walked out into the street and hailed a taxi to take them back to the hotel. On the way they discussed the possibilities and found the park where they had left the dragons. They relayed the news that Meredith had gone to one of her rigs in the East China Sea.

"Well that was a good piece of detective work boys..." she replied, commending them, "but it looks like all our efforts were in vain as we don't know the name of the rig!" She had underestimated her protector however as Angus recalled the something he had saw on the office wall in

Chennai. The name of the rig! It was named after her father; Charles Quinton Jones.

Chapter 20

'Light at the End of the Tunnel'

The sight of the gnawed bones and the stench within the chamber threatened to overpower Georgina, but the sound of scrabbling claws coming down the tunnel behind her brought her back to her senses. 'This was no time to go all girly!' she thought. Without hesitation she clambered into the left tunnel of the two in front of her and continued her flight from whatever was making the terrible noise. She was convinced that the beast was now gaining on her and she drove her body to produce as much effort as possible. The light from her brooch appeared to be brightening and she could see more and more of the yawning pothole ahead. Georgina felt as if she was a pawn in a giant game of chess, but she felt disadvantaged at not knowing all the rules and frustrated that she had no idea where she was going. It didn't seem fair; however she did not have time to ponder this and instead concentrated in putting more distance between herself and her pursuer. Another chamber presented a choice between two more tunnels and almost without thinking she chose the right hand path. She hoped that she could remember the way in reverse so she could find her way back out. Then she chastised herself for such a silly thought. Even if she did find the object she was supposed to search for, she might never get it out and she certainly could not go back the way she came as that would mean bumping into whatever hunted her. That was not a pleasant thought and by this stage her limbs were bone weary and even through her thick winter clothes she could feel blood trickling from her scraped elbows and knees. Georgina stopped for a rest and focused on Angus as she sat down on the stone floor, wondering where he was now and hoping that her father was out looking for them. These thoughts were cut short when she heard the now familiar snorting sound and she quickly realised that her pursuer still had her scent and was very much on her trail.

Georgina could hear the monster behind her and although exhausted in every fibre of her body, she pushed herself through the pain barrier to keep moving forward through the narrow space. The tunnel she was crawling through began to get very tight again and was so full of bends it made her progress very difficult. Now she could literally hear the beast scrabbling behind her and she feared for her life. The girl had never been in danger like this before; even on an adventure with Angus. Panic stricken she made an extra effort to push onwards. As she peered ahead she could see a glowing light and it reminded her of Krubera and the strange light that filled the underground cave system there. It seemed to fill the tunnel she crawled through in much the same way, and it was now bright enough to make her precious brooch redundant as a light source. Encouraged by this she pushed her body harder, hoping that the source of the light held sanctuary. The radiance of the light grew as she scrabbled on all fours through the tunnel and at last she saw that the path was straightening out in front of her. The far end was brilliantly illuminated so much that she was now blinded by it; her eyes had become so accustomed to the darkness her captors had forced her to endure. Still she pushed onwards, uncaring about anything other than escape from the hunter in the tunnel behind. She squinted forward and estimated that she still had a few metres to go before she would be clear of the tunnel, but suddenly she shot forward, gaining momentum as she fell from the tunnel mouth. Again the girl rolled forward, but the distance to the floor was not much and she bumped the back of her head as she rolled over and over on the rocky floor.

The young protector, battered and bruised, came to a halt in an ungainly heap. Every inch of her body ached and all she really wanted to do now was cry. Tears started to roll down her dirt covered cheeks, forging a clean pass through the grime that covered her pretty face.

"This is not the time'" she said to herself and wiping the tears away she mentally pulled herself together and sat up. Georgina rubbed the back of her head and her jaw dropped at what she saw in front of her. The chamber was filled with a strangely familiar and welcoming glow. The pursuing monster and her bumped head were suddenly forgotten as she surveyed the cavern she found herself sitting in. The light that seemed so familiar was indeed the same as the light which illuminated Krubera Cave, but was not quite as saturating as that which floods the home of the Cor Stan. This deep chamber was almost circular, but smaller than most of the caves in Krubera. Georgina blinked in disbelief as she looked around and her eyes widened in surprise. What she saw were many golden dragon statues wedged into the rock around the perimeter of the cavern. All of the dragons had glowing blue eyes and she guessed that these were the source of the light. Amazingly the eyes appeared to be made of Dragonore and her mind raced as a memory jumped up and down in her mind to be given some attention. She thought about the missing dragons from the Kew Garden's Pagoda and looking around it would be safe to assume she had discovered where they had vanished. What was really strange about the scene which confronted her was that the eyes were locked in a latticework of light beams. It reminded her of a security system that you might find in a museum which protected something of extreme value. That is when Georgina saw beyond the prism of beams to the object in the centre of the chamber. She stood on the path that led to the centre and she realised not all the eye beams covered the perimeter of the central area. Some were focused on a rock pedestal in the middle of the cavern. They completely enclosed the top of the pedestal in a tight latticework of beams. Something sat on the pedestal, but the object, whatever it was, could not be identified. Suddenly she heard a growl behind her and the girl span around. Brought abruptly back to the reality of her situation Georgina looked at the tunnel she had fallen from. The darkness hovered further inside the tunnel, driven back by the light from within the chamber and the girl watched in horror as the darkness took form and grew. The light glinted off milky white eyes and as the shape expanded the light revealed a snout with fanged teeth. The thing that had pursued her had not given up the chase and she stepped back looking around desperately for a way out. Stumbling over the rocky floor, Georgina could see that she was trapped in a dead end and now all her focus was on the hunter that had emerged from the darkness. No matter how much she wanted to she could not take her eyes off the creature for one moment. The beast continued to emerge into the pale blue light very slowly; its snout twitched and snorted as a long snakelike tongue flicked

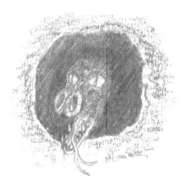 between razor sharp teeth. Her brain told her the creature was blind and she recognised the same white eyes that poor

Hereward used to have. Blinded by years underground in the darkness the beast searched for its prey by two senses; smell and taste. Fear suffocated Georgina's thoughts as the horror of her situation overwhelmed her!

Chapter 21

'Whipping Up a Storm'

Kadin watched the others around him as they flew yet further east in the direction of Shanghai. He felt exhilarated to be on an adventure with Angus and full of trepidation at what they might find ahead. Even if they found nothing, the trip was worth it just for the experience of travelling to different locations and if they had not made the effort they would surely not have recruited a new protector or found another hidden dragon. Best yet was the fact that this new dragon potentially held information about the lost Asian dragons and their disappearance from the world. From Hong Kong they had followed the coastline with the East China Sea on their right. The dragons had been suitably rested and had also managed to find some food to eat. Both he and Angus had decided not to ask any awkward questions about where the food had come from and that appeared to suit all concerned. The main thing was that they were on the way and it would hopefully bring them some answers as the replenished dragons were making good time. He looked across at Angus and Kadin felt that he looked troubled. In fact the Arabian dragon protector had thought this since he met Angus two days ago in

Dubai; but had not mentioned it as it did not seem polite. Over the past day Kadin had noticed that Pyrra watched her young protector closely and he sensed that she also knew that something was wrong. When he got the chance he resolved to speak to his friend and hoped that he could help in some way.

Soon they could see that the land opened up into a large circular bay and on the other side laid a vast city. Nehebkau now led as this was territory he knew well. The Asian dragon felt very sentimental as he neared the land of his youth. He pointed out Shanghai to the others and then waited for instructions as he was not really sure what they intended to do next. Before he had left Hong Kong, Angus had managed to find an internet cafe and had checked for pictures of the vessel they were looking for. He quickly found it along with many pictures of Meredith's late father. His portrait that Angus had seen in the Quinton-Jones family home had not really done him justice and as he looked much more formidable than in the painting. Now that he had the picture of the rig, named after Meredith's father, he hoped that spotting it would not be an issue. Unfortunately Angus could not have been further from the truth. The bay of Shanghai was massive and contained numerous vessels and waterways. They could see many vessels of various types dotted beneath them and how they were going to find one vessel in all of this was beyond him. Angus knew the others probably expected him to have the answers and his thoughts turned to Georgina and the vision of her prone body in that cell. Angus did not know if what the blue dragon had shown him was real or just a figment of his own imagination, but his resolve was strengthened by her plight and his determination to find her.

"If we split up, we will cover more ground!" he shouted to the others.

"What do you have in mind?" asked Pyrra.

"We can fly wider apart and starting from that end of the bay we can move east and check each of the vessels" replied Angus.

"That will take forever!" shouted Wymarc unhelpfully. The dragon was correct, but Angus could see no other way.

"I know, but I don't have any better ideas; do you?" he asked.

Wymarc shook his head and reluctantly had to agree with Angus that they did not have any choice but to search in a grid pattern from west to east. It was already late afternoon and darkness beckoned; making the task even more

difficult. Angus quickly deployed Wymarc to the north and
Kadin to the south, with Pyrra flying him in the centre. As
they wheeled left to start their run the young lad wondered
if his attempts to find Georgina would be seen as a child's
foolishness and naivety, but at this point of time he had
nothing else to hold on to and this was at least going to
rule some things out.

Their progress was not only hampered by darkness as
fog banks began to drift across the bay, further obscuring
their views. The dragons zigzagged across the search
zones, locating each vessel in turn as they confirmed the
type and name. They dared not use dragon time for this
activity for fear of missing a vessel and Angus shivered at
the thought of coming all this way and not finding what they
sought. After an hour they had almost reached the end of
the bay and Angus felt sure they had possibly missed it.
He had hoped one of the others would fly towards them at
any second, bringing news that they had indeed found it,
but that did not happen and Pyrra stolidly flew onwards.
The lights of Shanghai dropped away behind them and
Angus could see that the amount of vessels was dwindling
fast. He spotted a triangular vessel further ahead and it
looked very like the type of rig vessel they searched for.
The decks and leg structures were lit up like a Christmas

tree and he could see two boats towing the rig towards the open seas. He pointed excitedly and Pyrra dove in for a closer look. The darkness around the bottom of the hull made it difficult to see the name of the vessel as the lights were all above deck and the pair flew around the vessel in a circular flight path to try and find out if they had indeed located the Charles Quinton-Jones. Pyrra dropped further in height to get a closer look at the forward end and she hovered just above the towing wires between the tug boats and the rig.

"I think I see it..." pointed Angus, "There under the heli-deck!"

Pyrra tried to get a little closer but as she did so a wave smacked the bow of the rig and slowed the large vessel down. The resultant force dragged the tugs back and allowed the towing wires to slacken. As the wave gave way again the tugs sped forward whipping the metal towing cables upwards towards Pyrra.

Chapter 22

'Red Snapper'

The beast sniffed the air hungrily as it emerged from the darkness and into the pale blue light of the cavern. Georgina shook with fear as it slowly crept forward, front claw's tapping the rocks as it stepped. The tongue from the creature's mouth flicked left and right, the nostrils in the slimy snout were pointing upwards sniffing the air as it continued to track and advance on its quarry. It had waited for years for a decent meal and now it would be rewarded after such a long and patient sleep. It had survived for so long on the scant morsels that happened to fall its way but now it would eat fresh meat! And this meat smelt very fresh indeed and was now within reach.

Georgina watched in disgust and the creature revealed its true form. In her head a beastlike Minotaur stalked her through the tunnels although that now seemed silly as the real hunter slithered forward. The stench was repulsive and how this thing could smell anything above its own very unpleasant stench remained a mystery to Georgina. Petrified, the poor girl could not do anything else, but inch backwards and hope to escape past the beast, but that did not seem possible. Driven back by the advance of the monster she followed her only option and found herself backing into the middle of the chamber. The skin of the animal was pale, scaly and patchy. The patches were translucent in colour, but Georgina noted that the beast had been red at sometime in the past as layers of peeling skin drooped from various parts of its hide. It moved very slowly as if conserving energy, but then suddenly lunged several inches from the tunnel as if testing its prey. Georgina was too scared to make any noise now and her breathing was shallow and fast. She felt like a small rabbit being hunted by a wolf, with no hope of escape. Now that the beast had emerged further she could see that it was almost snakelike; however despite its serpent appearance she realised it was actually some kind of a dragon. Georgina remembered Angus describing the water dragon at Loch Ness and it seemed very likely to her that this dragon was perhaps also a Wyrm. It stopped for a second and tasted the air with its tongue and then froze in one position. Suddenly darted forward and snapped the air with alligator like jaws. Georgina stumbled back as the sharp fangs snapped shut within inches of her legs. Saliva sprayed from the jaws and a drip of the putrid moisture landed on her feet. She had fallen back and pushing herself back up she stumbled a few more inches out of reach. As she did so, rancid breath hit her face as the ancient Wyrm slowly began to follow.

The tail of the dragon had now emerged and Georgina could now see the full size of the Wyrm; flicking and twitching with excitement as it closed in on her. The beast continued to advance and for a second Georgina thought that she could perhaps reason with it.

"I'm a protector... from the SSDP!" she shouted, fear dripping from her voice.

The Wyrm stopped and cocked its head to one side as if considering what was said. Georgina thought that perhaps it had worked and that the dragon now realised she was a friend. She had held her breath after speaking to the dragon and the young protector exhaled in response to her protesting lungs. As if triggered by this, the Wyrm sprang forward again snapping as it lunged. Georgina stumbled to one side narrowly dodging the slobbering jaws and as she did so her foot rolled over a rock and sent her sprawling backwards to the rocky floor. The girl froze as the beast sniffed the air a few feet from her prone body. Georgina had never felt so vulnerable, but summoning strength from somewhere deep inside, she slowly and extremely quietly moved back on all fours. All the while she watched the mouth of the dragon, ready to dodge should the vicious fangs attack again. Her hand came across a stone and she picked it up and tossed it behind the Wyrm. The beast immediately spun its head and moved in that direction to investigate; forked tongue tasting the air. Georgina could not take her eyes from the ancient beast as she scrabbled back away from her tormentor. In the process of doing so she dislodged some more rubble and the noise spun the dragon and she watched in terror as it advanced; all the while making the same strange gurgling sounds she had heard in the tunnels. The Wyrm closed in and sensing victory it lunged above her; huge teeth poised above her for one final and fatal attack.

Chapter 23

'The Charles Quinton-Jones'

Angus gripped hard as Pyrra wheeled sideways; the
wire swept up past her left wing and the young protector
was convinced it had hit her. The green dragon spun in the
air trying to regain control, her tail flailing into the choppy
sea a few feet below them. The boy held on for his life as
he did not fancy his chances in the freezing water;
especially in the foggy darkness. The wires continued to
bounce under the strain of the forces acting on them and
the tugs slowly powered on; unaware of the drama
because Pyrra was invisible. At last the dragon regained
control and with a final flap righted her body.

"Are you okay Pyrra?" asked Angus.

"I'm fine..." she replied, "but it was a close one!"
Angus loosened his grip slightly and looked at the rig
again; finally finding the name of the vessel.

"It's not the right one Pyrra" he said quietly.
The dragon did not reply but simply climbed higher into the
sky to avoid the oncoming vessel.

"I'm sorry Pyrra... Maybe this was a bad idea" said
Angus.

Pyrra turned to look him in the eye she seemed to consider the lad for a second or two before answering.

"Do you think I would be here if I did not believe in you Angus?" she asked.

The young protector felt heartened by this and he smiled and continued to look for the vessel they sought.

The pair scanned the seas below for any other vessels and Angus noticed a plume of flames in the distance. As Pyrra flew further more plumes appeared and then the source of the plume became clearer. The flames were emitting from towers and the towers were attached to rigs. The green dragon did not need to be told to take a closer look as she too had seen them and had already trimmed her wings to descend in that direction. Angus recalled the multitude of Oil and Gas structures he had seen in the Arabian Gulf while on the way to Dubai; these were similar structures and just as numerous. They were joined by Wymarc and obviously he had not been successful in finding the vessel either. It appeared to Angus that they had no choice but to go in for a closer look. The first few structures were permanent platforms, clearly placed to endure a sustained period of operation. A variety of vessels were moored near or alongside the platforms and all of them were lit up even more than the vessel they had seen earlier. They circled around one of the flares as it spouted flames high into the air and although they maintained some distance Angus could still feel the heat as it radiated outwards. He looked towards the next fiery plume and noticed it was partially obscured by some sort of latticework. Drawing closer the framework became clearer and he could see that it was very similar to the triangular vessel that had earlier threatened to end their adventure. Angus watched as Pyrra drew closer to the lights under the heli-deck and they both saw what they had been looking for. Painted on the back of the grey hull was the large red lettering of Meredith's company and directly underneath was her father's name 'CHARLES QUINTON-JONES'.

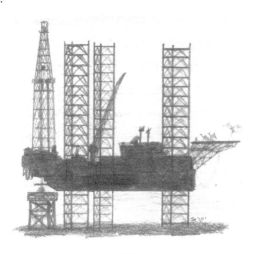

They had finally located the correct vessel and Wymarc volunteered to go and fetch Nehebkau and Kadin. As he disappeared into the darkness, Pyrra circled the jack-up rig and surveyed the decks for activity. The structure was triangular in shape and had three long legs. The legs were made of steel tubes and were formed into square frameworks that went through large holes in the deck. Angus could see from the picture he found earlier and the real thing that the legs appeared to be held in place by large frames attached to the deck and he assumed that these frames somehow powered the legs up and down. This meant that the vessel could travel from place to place and jack-up out of the water as it pushed the legs onto the seabed. At least that is how he saw and it all seemed plausible to him since the legs he looked at now were considerably shorter than the picture he had in his pocket and this was confirmed when Pyrra flew under the hull. The underneath of the jack-up rig was lightly covered in barnacles from being in the water, but the whole vessel now sat so high from the water that they could fly beneath and out through the other side. The dragon climbed again for another circuit over the structure and Angus began to notice other details. At the end where the flare burned he could see that part of the structure had been extended out over a small fixed platform. The protector could see men in boiler suits and hard hats moving around on that part of the structure. Above the men was a tall tower and he could see long thin pipes being fed into the tower and placed on top of each other, end to end. He watched mesmerised as the end of the pipe would lower down before a new piece was attached. This operation was repeated time and again and when they passed by a second time he could see that the pipe extended down through the small platform below. He realised that they must be drilling and he wished he could take a closer look as it was obvious the rig was in full operation. At the opposite side of the rig was a large building that wrapped around the opening for the leg at that end. Angus could see a control room on top and a heli-deck overhung the forward end of the vessel.

It was not long before the others rejoined them and Pyrra had decided that she would land on the vacant helicopter deck. They dismounted and the lads stood by the dragons as they discussed what to do next.

"Remember that you will be visible as soon as you leave our side, so be careful" reminded Pyrra.
Angus acknowledged this and told them his plan.

"I saw a couple of men walking around the main deck below and I think they were patrolling so we will need to be careful not to bump into them" he explained to Kadin.

"Where do you think we should start?" asked the Arab boy.

"We can enter through the doors there, start on this level and work our way down" he replied. "I will take this side and you take that one" he added indicating Kadin to the left.

They walked off the heli-deck via some stairs near the white building and Angus saw a sign that read 'Living Quarters'.

Both lads walked quietly down the metal steps which were made up of silver coloured steel gratings. As they descended down under the level of the heli-deck Angus could see that it was supported by large tubular steel pillars that connected with the living quarters and the deck far below. The whole of the helicopter deck hung over what Angus assumed was the front of the vessel as he had already witnessed one of these vessels earlier that evening. The thought of that wire slicing past Pyrra's wing made him shudder and he was just happy that she was unhurt by the incident. When they reached the bottom of the stairs they split up as Angus had indicated, each walking along a long metal gangway that went around the outside of the living quarters. As Angus headed for the door on his left he noticed more stairs leading down to the next level and counted three levels in total. He hoped they would not need to search the whole building as it was going to be risky enough without having to do that. Once at the door he peered into a small window situated in the upper half. He could see a brightly lit corridor with several more doors on either side and at the far end another door similar to the one he now stood behind. The young lad grabbed the long metal handle and lifted it upwards. The heavy watertight door squealed at the hinges as he slowly pulled it open. Angus cringed at the noise it made and when it was open enough he squeezed through pausing to see if anyone would investigate the noise. After a few seconds he relaxed as it appeared his entrance had not alerted the crew, but then he realised he would still need to close the portal again and he winced as he pulled it shut with a bang. He pushed the handle down again and several rods on the inside of the door slotted outwards from the centre of the door and locked into the outer frame. He waited again to ensure that no-one had heard and then he began to look at the doors along the corridor. It appeared that most of them were cabins and he guessed they were for crew as each had a number with the words 'TWO MAN CABIN' on the door. Angus decided not to enter these cabins and he continued along the corridor until he found something more suitable.

Kadin had entered via another watertight door and he too stood holding his breath after he closed and locked it behind him. He turned to read the label on the first door which clearly stated it was a 'utility cupboard'. He had a quick peek inside and as he had guessed it was full of cleaning equipment. He closed the door and continued to search when he heard a door opening up ahead. He heard laughter and a man stepped out from a doorway several metres away. Fortunately the man had stepped only halfway over the threshold as he was still conversing with someone else inside the room. Kadin did not hear what they were talking about, nor did he care as he quickly tried to find a hiding place. Grabbing the handle to the utility room door, the Arab lad only just managed to get inside as the man turned around. Kadin listened from inside the cramped space as the man's footsteps continued past his hiding place and out through the heavy watertight door.

Angus had found a couple of offices and bravely taken a look inside but had found nothing that helped. If he was being honest with himself he did not even know what he was looking for and he even wondered if Georgina might be on the vessel somewhere. The only thing he could do was keep looking and see if he could find any sign of Meredith and he was positive the crazy heiress was the key to finding Georgina. Having reached the end of the corridor he decided to try his luck on the next level and he looked through the window to see if the coast was clear. He could see some men working on the deck below and taking a big risk, he opened the door.

After a minute or so, Kadin decided to risk looking out from his hiding place. He felt really scared sneaking around a strange vessel thousands of miles from home, but at the same time he felt exhilarated. The coast was clear and he quickly stepped out and jogged quietly along the corridor; checking name plates as he went. After exhausting all of them he realised that he would have to go down to the next level, but unlike Angus he could not force himself to exit into the exposed area above the deck. He turned about and went back to the door he had already used.

The door closed and Angus locked the handle in place; successfully doing so without any excessive noise. All the while he watched the main deck for any signs that the men working below had detected him. Very carefully he walked to the stairs and began to descend to the next level. The men appeared to be constructing something on the deck and all three were too busy to notice the young boy two landings above them. Angus opened the watertight door as silently as he could and quickly slipped inside. Again a long corridor stretched in front of him but this time he could see another branch off to the left. The doors on this level were marked as one man cabins and he even found one that stated 'Rig Manager' on the door. He guessed that was the equivalent of a captain and continued on whilst he checked any that showed potential. When Angus reached the branch section it turned out to be another corridor and he decided to try his luck down there. As Angus walked he could hear voices and he immediately started to creep more stealthily towards a door that had light shining through a glass window. The window filled half the door and in large bold letters it stated 'RADIO ROOM' on the glass. Angus crept up to the door and peered over the edge of the glass and into the room. A man sat at one of many consoles with his back to the door and another sat writing at a desk. Both were too busy to notice Angus but neither was talking and Angus realised that it was a radio that he could hear from inside the room; however it was not music that played. Unlike a commercial radio station this was a shipping communication radio and he could hear the chatter of people talking in what he guessed was one of the Chinese languages.

The door plate in front of Kadin told him that this was yet another 'two man' cabin and he was almost ready to give up when he found a room labelled 'VIP CABIN'. Hope rose within him as he tried the door handle, but it was soon dashed when it turned out to be locked. Frustrated at his lack of progress, he decided to try and find Angus. Unsure of where his partner in adventure was, Kadin saw another passage off to his left and decided to investigate. He turned the corner and immediately jumped back as he walked straight into someone standing there. It took him a couple of seconds to realise the person he saw was Angus and he smiled at his friend.

"Sorry..." whispered Angus, "you okay?"

"I am now that I know you are not a guard!" replied Kadin.

"I haven't found anything yet... you?" asked Angus. Kadin nodded and beckoned Angus to follow him.

Both boys investigated the VIP room together and Kadin demonstrated that they needed a key. Angus smiled and this time it was he who led Kadin back to the Radio Room. Once there he pointed to the wall above the man still writing at the desk. A rack of keys were hung on the wall and Angus indicated that he thought the keys might be there. The only problem was that the office was occupied. They decided the best way to get the keys was to cause a distraction.

"You stay hidden and watch for the guard leaving" said Angus. "Once you see them leaving; go and get the key."

As fast as he could Angus made his way back out to the forward side of the quarters and returned to the heli-deck. He quickly told the dragons what was going on and he enlisted their help. The plan was to cause a problem that would draw the men out of the Radio Room. The only issue was that, for once, Angus could not think of anything.

"Don't worry..." said Pyrra, "Leave it to me!" Without another word she flicked out her wings and disappeared over the top of the building.

Sitting patiently across the corridor from the Radio Room, Kadin waited behind the door of an empty office. He listened intently for any sign of the distraction that would draw out the men, but nothing happened. After several minutes he was beginning to get nervous about the whole plan and he was about to go and look for Angus when he heard something. The two men were speaking very animatedly about a problem with the radio system, but he could not tell what they were talking about. He heard the door of the Radio Room open and hurried footsteps disappear along the corridor. He did not need to be told twice and seized his chance to get into the room. Kadin ran to the cabinet with the keys. Having noted the door number earlier he quickly searched the key labels to find the correct one. The first rack checked, he started on the next, but then he heard the watertight door opening again and his search became more frantic as he realised that the men were coming back.

Chapter 24

'The Silver Claw'

Instinctively Georgina shrieked and raised her arms over her head in an effort to fend off the attack of the dragon. The crunching bite of razor sharp teeth she expected never came and instead she smelt the foul air of the Wyrm's breath. She dared not look but at the same time the girl needed to know why the fowl beast had spared her life. 'Perhaps he is just toying with me; like a cat does with a mouse' she thought. Moving her arms slightly she unclenched her fists and opened her eyes just a fraction. Georgina peeked out from the crook of her arm to see what had happened to her assailant. To her amazement the dragon hovered above her in mid air; teeth poised to bite down on her. Georgina took a deep breath through her mouth so she would not smell the foul odour of the dragon's breath. The Wyrm closed its mouth and glided back from his quarry clearly agitated at not getting the meal it desired. Georgina was confused and she could not work out why the beast had not finished off what must have been easy prey. She sat up and looked around her to see where she had fallen and that is when Georgina realised what had saved her. She had struggled to escape her attacker and as with most prey she had not really paid much attention to where she was going; her only concern being escape. When she stumbled and fell back she had penetrated the outer ring of the light blue eye beams. And it was these same eye beams that appeared to have stopped the dragon. Apparently the Wyrm could not pass them and Georgina thanked whoever had positioned them there for saving her life. 'At least for now anyway!' she thought as it became apparent that the dragon was staying between her and the only way out.

As the dragon paced to and fro on the edge of the beams of light, Georgina began to study her surroundings a little more closely. She had the time now as it did not look like she was going anywhere. She stepped towards the foot of the plinth and could now see that the base was made of stone and had symbols similar to those she had seen on the door at Calmor Castle. Although she felt safe at the foot of the plinth, Georgina kept her eye on her tormentor. She was still totally baffled as to why the Wyrm would not attack her but it was something she would not complain about and she hoped it would last. She turned her attention to the object on the pedestal which was now a bit easier to see. It appeared to be a silver object and it looked like a blade of some sort. Around it the beams of light were so intense that she could not put her hand through without breaking a beam. Again she was reminded of a security system in a museum and she took a step forward and tried to penetrate the light beam cage. Like the Wyrm that fidgeted impatiently behind her, Georgina found she could not penetrate the defences of the pedestal and the object remained out of her reach. The young protector was sure that this was the object she was supposed to retrieve but she was stumped as to how she would be able to complete the task. Even if she could take it, she would not escape past the hungry beast that had stalked her throughout the tunnel system. Georgina sat on the floor; bleeding and bruised she had never felt such despair in all her life. Thinking of her father and how frantic he would be with worry she began to sob quietly into her hands. As she cried the Wyrm made a whining noise as if joining the girl in her sorrow. Georgina looked at the ancient and scabby dragon.

"No!" she said, more to herself. "I am not giving in that easily and you are not going to eat me!"
The young protector lent forward to stand up and as she did one of the beams diverted onto her brooch.

"Now that was interesting" she said to herself.

Georgina stood up and moved back to the intricate web of beams linking with each other. She took off her brooch and held it towards one of the beams. Suddenly a beam cast out a link to the Dragonore mounted in the eye of the dragon brooch she wore. She could not pass through the beams when she tried before but somehow she managed to pass through the outer beams when the dragon could not. She looked more closely at the Wyrm and she realised how decrepit the poor creature looked. The dragon did not even have any jewels on its chest like normal dragons and that is when a thought struck her.

"That's it Georgina..." she said to herself as she turned to the pedestal again, "you silly girl!"
The cage of light was impenetrable but if she provided the key to unlock the cage then she could get in. Her brooch was the key and she unpinned and moved her hand holding the brooch towards the beams. The light intensified as her hand neared the light, but she found she could cross the barrier. With the dragon brooch in her left hand almost like a pass key, she met no resistance and she reached onto the plinth and grasped the protected object.

The beams of light had increased so much that she had to close her eyes to the brightness. Her hand clasped around the object and she pulled it from the cage of beams. Suddenly she heard a wailing roar and the Dragonore eye beams around the plinth suddenly disappeared like a candle flame being blown out. Like an alarm system the noise penetrated every inch of the cavern and even the Wyrm shrank back in fear. As she watched, two dragons began to morph from two of the statues that had protected the plinth. The beams had disappeared but the eyes of the small statues blazed brightly. The dragons had only half materialised, staying in a ghostly form the likes of which Georgina had never seen before. The connection to the object had been broken and both the wraithlike dragons considered Georgina before wailing again and taking off. They flew frantic circuits around the cavern as if looking for the way out.

"Wait!" she cried as the pair circled her head
They spun around the girl faster and faster until she could not make anything out but a blurred streak. They circled closer to the girl and fearing for her life she dropped to her knee gripping the object to her chest.

"Leave me alone!" she shouted above the din.
The ethereal dragons appeared to hear her pleas and shot past the Wyrm and into the tunnel beyond.

Georgina looked up and opened her eyes now that the wailing had stopped. Whatever they were they were not

happy to see her and it obviously had something to do with
the object she held. The young girl opened up her hand
and in it she held a Silver Claw. It had no markings on it at

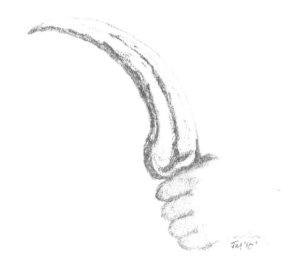

all and looked very much like a claw she saw in the Natural
History Museum last year. Like that of a Velociraptor, but
much larger. She turned the claw in her hands inspecting it
as it shown in the dim light of the outer beams. A gurgling
noise brought her back to reality and she remembered the
Wyrm which hovered at the only exit. Retrieving the Silver
Claw was all in vain as Georgina could not get past her
captor and she would die there after all. The frustration
welled up inside her until she could no longer hold it back.

"I wish you would just go away and leave me alone" she screamed at the beast.

At once, the dragon turned its back on her, dropped to the ground and slithered up the tunnel. Stunned at what she just witnessed Georgina waited for a few moments thinking the Wyrm would surely come back, but was surprised when it did not. After several minutes the young girl tentatively stepped away from the safety of the beams wondering how on earth she was going to get out of this nightmare.

Chapter 25

'Breadcrumbs'

Kadin could hear the heavy steel watertight door creak on rusty hinges and desperately he searched the rack for the key he needed. Unconsciously he had started to move away from the rack and nearer the door as his subconscious told him he was going to get caught. But they needed the key and Angus was counting on him. A voice shouted from outside and whoever was at the doorway, began to call back.

"What did you say?"

The Arab boy decided that he could not wait a second more and turned to leave; only to spin immediately back to the rack of keys. 'Was that the correct number?' he thought as he quickly scanned the spot that had caught his eye. The steel door creaked again; there it was! Kadin quickly picked up the key and ran to the door of the Radio Room. Without pause he dove across the passageway and into the room opposite just as the two men turn the corner. From the safety of his hiding place Kadin listens to the men as they walked back to their duties.

"What do you think caused that aerial to bend like that?" asked one of the men.

"I don't know but it's the darndest thing I ever saw!" replied the other.

Kadin waited for a few minutes and then checked to see if the coast was clear. The door to the Radio Room was closed and keeping low he slipped through the merest of gaps in the door to his hiding place. The Arab lad moved off to meet with Angus at the VIP cabin.

Angus had been anxiously watching through the door window from the other end of the corridor and had seen the two men return to the Radio Room. He hoped that Kadin was okay and was over the moon when he saw his Arab friend turn the corner. The protectors met in the middle of the corridor next to the VIP room.

"You got it then?" asked Angus smiling.

"I am pleased to say that my mission was a success!" replied Kadin, grinning as he held up his trophy.

They used the key to get inside and realised that they were indeed inside Meredith's cabin. The decor was much plusher than the rest of the rig and Angus noted a picture of her father sat on a desk at the far wall. Three small windows lined the far wall and the furnishings were grander and more ornate than any he had seen in the previous cabins. The desk was covered in papers and Angus immediately moved in that direction as Kadin began to look elsewhere in the cabin. The paperwork was piled in neat bundles and the young protector quickly scanned the top sheets to see if anything was worth his attention. They all appeared to be technical documents of some sort and procedures for stuff he had no clue about so he left them alone.

"Did you find anything?" asked Kadin from the other side of the room.

"Not yet... you?" asked Angus in turn.

"Nothing, but I still have this cabinet to look through" replied Kadin.

Angus continued to scan the desk for any clue and opened the top drawer to see if anything worthwhile was inside. Nothing of note caught his eye and he closed it again to start on the next drawer down. Then he noticed what looked like the edge of a map under one of the piles of paperwork. He abandoned the drawer he was about to open and picked up the pile of papers and placed them carefully to one side.

"I think I've found something" he said to Kadin. Almost immediately the Arab boy was at his side as Angus opened out the map. It was a Chinese map, but Angus could make out the coastline and clearly marked on the map was a small circle just off the coast of Shanghai. He assumed that it was the position of the Charles Quinton-Jones and that was when he noted another circle over an area to the north west of Shanghai near a large lake. Next to it was written 'Lake Palace' and Angus pointed it out to Kadin.

"Do you suspect that is where Meredith is?" asked Kadin.

"I think it could be... but there is only one way to find out!" replied Angus as he folded the map and tucked it inside his jacket pocket.

Chapter 26

'Job Done'

The cavern somehow felt cold and empty after the flurry of activity. Georgina struggled to work out exactly what had happened when she retrieved the claw from the pedestal, and she did not know if the two ghostly dragons were in fact real; but it did appear that she had triggered some sort of alarm and now that the Wyrm had wriggled off, she was not going to hang around waiting to see who else might show up. If someone was going to be upset by the theft of the object then they could take it up with Meredith. Once more the girl steadied her resolve and began to crawl out of the cavern with the Silver Claw tucked inside her thick jacket for safekeeping.

The young female protector tried desperately to remember the way she had come, but despite her best efforts she repeatedly hit dead ends and kept having to return to the previous junction. Georgina wove her way through the maze of tunnels, all the while wondering where the two golden dragons had shot off to in such a hurry and above all, what had become of the Wyrm. Slowly and steadily she crawled back the same way and several times she thought she could hear the Wyrm scurry off in the opposite direction whenever she caught up with it. This suited the girl very well indeed and she pondered the reason behind its strange behaviour. 'Perhaps it is because I have the Silver Claw' she thought; but two more wrong turnings soon focused her concentration again. The darkness began to oppress her again and the light from her brooch was failing as she moved further from the central source of the Dragonore below. It was not a pleasant situation and Georgina longed to see daylight and freedom. She was now so fatigued that she could hardly stand and her body was bruised and bleeding. All she wanted to do was to get home and it was the only thing that drove her onwards. It took an age to navigate through the tunnels and she had no idea of time or how long she had been down inside the mountain. At long last Georgina felt encouraged as she felt a slight breeze coming from one of the tunnels in front of her. Heartened by this she followed the fresher air and arrived at the point where she had fallen from the first tunnel. That was when she realised she could not get out as it was far too steep and slippery for her to climb; even if there were footholds. She stood on her tip-toes and peered up the shaft she had originally been forced into. The young protector knew she did not have the strength to pull her body up into the tunnel, let alone climb up it to the surface. She tried anyway and almost managed to get her torso inside when her grip slipped and her hopes were dashed completely when she hit the floor below. The girl started to sob uncontrollably as realisation dawned on her that she would probably never escape this death trap. Anger welled up from inside her as she thought of her captors above.

"I hate you Meredith!" she shrieked at the top of her voice and then she screamed incoherently as loud as she could; the sound echoing all around her and along the tunnels. The echo's died away and silence returned. Nothing had changed and she was still trapped. She began to cry once more into her hands as thoughts of her father and of Angus overwhelmed her.

"This is not the way it was supposed to end" she said as she swiped at something touching her head. Suddenly her hand flicked a soft object and she immediately jumped with fright, thinking the Wyrm had somehow sneaked up on her, but it was nowhere in sight. What she did find was a climbing rope and its red and yellow snakelike pattern dangled invitingly in front of her, just within reach.

Minutes later Georgina was pulled from the tunnel she had entered so unwillingly at the start of her perilous task.

And she had no sooner collapsed on the frozen grass in front of Meredith when the mad woman seized the young protector.

"Tell me you have it?" she demanded.

Georgina was too exhausted and sore to argue with her and she pushed her hand inside her jacket and retrieved the Silver Claw. Meredith grabbed it triumphantly and started cackling like a hyena.

"I have it..." she preened. "Oh how they will all regret embarrassing me!"

Georgina squinted up at the crazed woman standing before her. The sunlight hurt her eyes, but she could see that although the claw was in fact made from silver, it also looked like real bone.

"I underestimated you girly, you have done well!" said Meredith looking down at her captive. "What's that you say?"

Georgina lay on the grass and tried to ask to be taken home, but her words were almost indiscernible. Meredith just smiled insanely at her.

"Of course you will go home my dear, but not until I am ready to return!" she replied.

"What about Angus?" Georgina asked.

She had been barely able to get the words out and the girl looked about her half expecting to see Angus tied up to a tree or something. The heiress realised what the girl was thinking.

"Oh I'm sorry my dear... did I give you the impression I had Angus captive as well?" sneered Meredith. "Thanks to you, Georgina, I will have him as soon as we get back to England, and you will make marvellous bait!"

Chapter 27

'Chinese Surprise'

Angus looked at the map again and wondered what awaited them at their next destination. He felt confident that they were getting nearer to Meredith and he hoped that would lead him to Georgina, but he still doubted his instincts and feared it would be yet another bread crumb left behind by Meredith. The map had been marked with a small circle in an area west of Shanghai and Angus realised that it was a long way from the city, but Pyrra and the other dragons had insisted that they travelled without a break. He was worried about them as they had flown so far in the last two days with only a short rest in Hong Kong. By the time they had found the rig on Sunday night it was already midnight and although he and Kadin did not take too long to find the map; they had not left until the small hours of Monday morning. It had not taken long for the two lads to exit from the rig, but when they did get into the air Angus was sure he heard alarms go off again. He hoped that it was nothing to do with their visit; however it was too late to worry about it now.

It had taken them about three hours to travel to the lake and the young protector sensed that the others were as keen as he was to see Georgina returned to the SSDP unharmed and he hoped their faith in him would not be misplaced. The sun was already beginning to rise behind them when he spotted mountains and the large lake behind them. The sunlight reflected off of the lakes surface and Angus could see that it stretched for some distance beyond a city situated on the western shore; the city itself stretched along the banks of a river. Both boys and dragons were exhausted from the exertions of the last two days and he could not believe they had completed so much flying and visited so many countries on this trip. The only thing Angus was sure of was that he was beginning to trust more and more in the mysterious dark blue dragon from his dreams.

"Over there Pyrra" shouted Angus after consulting the map again.

The name of the lake was Chao and the only thing he knew about the palace was that it was called the 'Lake Palace' because of its situation. Pyrra descended towards the mountains and soon they were flying over lush green trees and snow covered summits. The palace stood on the western face of one of the mountains and as they approached Angus guessed this was to take advantage of uninterrupted views of the lake. As it was winter the lake was partially frozen over, being too big to freeze completely. Soon the palace came into view and the young lad could see lights along the outside walls. He did not get much of a chance to see much more of the internal layout before they landed in a small clearing. They boys jumped to the ground and went to have a look through the tree line that faced the main gate.

"Who would have thought we'd end up here!" said Angus rhetorically.

Kadin did not reply but the look he returned told Angus that the Arab boy shared his thoughts. Neither of them expected to be contemplating sneaking into an ornate looking palace set facing a large lake, many miles west of Shanghai in China!

Once the boys disembarked they were visible and they felt quite exposed in open ground. Cautiously they made their way towards the fine palatial complex with strong walls surrounding inner buildings. There was not a soul around and it was also rather cold so Angus pulled his hood over his head and zipped up his jacket all the way to his chin. The boys followed the mulberry trees a little and managed to discover that the gate was firmly closed. They did not go any closer as they did not want to give themselves away to anyone possibly watching and they had no idea whom they might encounter. Angus smiled to think Georgina would find this all very exciting and the thought of Georgina made him refocus. Meanwhile Kadin had tried to find a way into the palace buildings by any visible means, but came back dejected.

"Any luck?" asked Angus already knowing the answer.

"No my friend... I am afraid we cannot get in through any doors" replied the young Arab boy.

"This is useless. Let's go back to the dragons and ask them to scope the place out!" said Angus shivering in the chilly morning air.

It did not take them too long to find Pyrra, Nehebkau and Wymarc deep in discussion.

"What's up guys?" said Angus as he approached.

"Did you find anything?" replied the dragon ignoring his question.

"No, we didn't. The gates are locked' answered Angus.

"Wymarc wants to fly into the compound and look for Georgina, but I think we need to be a little more careful!" explained Pyrra.

"That sounds like a good idea. Maybe you'll find something" said Angus.

"You see, we should go and find Georgina!" said Wymarc triumphantly.

"That's not what he said, Wymarc!" said Pyrra tersely. "He only said we should go and have a look."

"I think that Pyrra is correct. We should just take a look and nothing more for now" added Nehebkau.

Wymarc considered the two dragons for a few seconds and then conceded.

"Okay. We'll be back soon; stay here and wait until we return" said Pyrra.

The three dragons unfurled their wings and took off to get an aerial view of the palace and to look for any clue or signs of life. Angus and Kadin watched the dragons fly off over the trees towards the palace.

"In shaa'Allah they find something" said Kadin.

"Yeah me to!" replied Angus.

Suddenly they heard a voice behind them in what Angus assumed was Chinese. Both protectors spun around in surprise!

Chapter 28

'Yingjie'

At first Angus and Kadin were confused as they could not see anyone. Then a teenage boy stepped out from behind a tree. Again he repeated the words he had said before, but since neither Kadin nor Angus spoke any Chinese they could not answer. The boy walked towards them and was about the same age as both the protectors; although Angus decided he was perhaps a little older since he was a few inches taller. Again the lad asked something in Chinese and both he and Kadin just looked at each other blankly. The young lad stood squarely in front of them with his hands on his hips as the lads weighed each other up.

"I said what are you doing here?" asked the taller lad finally.
His English was almost perfect and Angus quickly recovered his composure to answer.

"What business is it of yours?" replied Angus defensively.
The young protector was not sure just how long the Chinese lad had been in the trees. He could not have seen

the dragons but he might have heard Kadin and himself talking to them.

"When you trespass on my land then I make it my business!" replied the lad becoming more aggressive. Angus weighed up this answer and looked the boy up and down. It could be possible he was telling the truth but judging by his clothes he did not look like he or his family were that wealthy and something about his manner made Angus believe he was lying.

"Well if that's the case you had better get the gates open and call someone for help; hadn't you?" replied Angus with a slight smile.

This appeared to deflate the lad slightly and for a moment or two both boys stared at each other defiantly. The Chinese lad's posture relaxed and his manner became more amiable.

"Okay I confess, I am not from around here..." he smiled, "but tell me... where did the dragons fly off to?" Both Angus and Kadin looked at each other. 'It was bad enough for the dragons to have been spotted in India by someone, but to have it happen here as well is just unbelievable!' thought Angus trying to figure out what to say next. Clearly this lad had Dragonore and Angus wondered if he was even aware of it.

"Before I answer you; I need to know if you have any small stones on you... if you can show me that, then I will tell you all you need to know!" replied Angus.

Cautiously the boy pulled a pendant from under his winter coat and showed it to the two protectors.

"My grandfather gave me this and I did not wear it until he went missing a few weeks ago!" said the boy.

The light blue stone shone brilliantly as it dangled from the lads hand and Angus realised his own Dragonore felt slightly warmer against his chest. He removed the string from around his own neck and took his Dragonore from the safety of the pouch he always kept it in. The stone that started the revival of the SSDP; his stone, glowed brightly as he held it between thumb and forefinger.

"I do not understand... what does this mean?" asked the tall lad.

"I will explain that, but it's a strange coincidence that we're here to try and find a friend of ours who has also disappeared" replied Angus.

"Where are you from?" asked the lad, looking intrigued.

"My name is Angus and I'm from the UK and this is Kadin from Dubai" answered Angus after deciding to trust the boy a little more.

"That is a long way to travel... that must be a good friend!" added the lad, "My name is Yingjie and I am here for my Grandfather You Longwei; I believe he is held captive inside that palace!"

"We're tracking a woman I think is responsible for the disappearance of our friend Georgina and we think the woman is in there too." explained Angus, "This is bizarre!"

"Indeed and I think we would do well to work together" added Kadin.

"Kadin's right, but first I need to explain a few things..." said Angus before going on to tell how they had got there and who they thought was inside. The young protector also went on to explain about the SSDP and the dragons.

"So that's why we have Dragonore and that's why you could see the dragons!" finished Angus.
Yingjie looked stunned and tried several times to say something, but from the looks of things he was not sure what to say next.

"So tell me how you got your Dragonore again?" asked Angus, helping him out.

"The pendant was given to me by my grandfather, but I just thought it was nothing..." replied the boy looking at the stone in his hand with new eyes. "I have never seen a dragon before and I did not know he had given me such a wonderful and powerful gift!"

"How do you know he's been brought here?" asked Kadin.

"When I came back from the town all I found was this" replied Yingjie holding out a long smoking pipe, "He would never leave it behind!"

"So did you follow him here?" asked Angus.

The lad appeared worried by this question as if he did want to answer.

"Well... it's silly really... you'll laugh" replied Yingjie.

"Believe me Yingjie... after what I've seen; I could believe almost anything is possible!" replied Angus earnestly.

"It came to me in a dream and I was shown the way here!" explained Yingjie.

Angus grinned and immediately the Chinese lad thought he was being ridiculed.

"You see... I knew you would laugh!"

"No sorry you misunderstand me Yingjie... I'm smiling because I have similar dreams!" explained Angus quickly.

Yingjie looked for honesty in Angus' answer and when he saw it in the young protector's face he smiled and held out his hand.

"Call me Ying" he said, shaking Angus by the hand, "It's my nickname."

The boys began to talk about what Ying knew of the palace and how they could possibly get inside.

The dragons had flown around the palace walls as they looked for any sign of life. No-one appeared to be around although Pyrra realised it was still early morning. They dived down for a closer look and as they approached the main buildings Pyrra's Dragonore began to glow fiercely.

"Quickly we need to gain height or we will give away our presence!" she called to the other two dragons.

They soared back up and away from the palace.

"We must go and investigate... it could be Georgina inside!" shouted Wymarc.

"No Wymarc! It was no human. I felt it was a dragon!" she replied, "Something is wrong here and we need to get back to the boys... let's go!"

With that she flicked her wings and began to fly back to the spot where they had left Angus and Kadin.

The Chinese lad Yingjie admitted that he had been trying to work out a way to get inside for a day. He had not seen anyone enter or leave in all that time. His grandfather was all the family he had left and he felt bad for leaving him that day.

"He is just an old man and I should have looked after him better..." he explained to the protectors, "he just tells me he can look after himself... but he's almost 96!"

"Wow... 96... No way!" replied Angus.

Ying went on to explain how his grandfather was always telling him to look to the old ways and that they were both born during the year of the dragon which was deemed to be very lucky indeed.

"Do you think your grandfather knows about the Dragonore?" asked Angus.

"I don't know... perhaps" he replied thoughtfully.

The Chinese lad wondered what else his grandfather had not told him. Suddenly they heard the flapping of large wings overhead and they looked up to greet the returning dragons. What surprised them was that only Pyrra and Nehebkau came back and there was no sign of Georgina's dragon.

"Wymarc decided to go straight inside without waiting for the rest of us!" explained a very disgruntled Pyrra. "We were on our way here when he said something about not wasting any more time!"

"He was convinced that there was no danger in there even though Pyrra felt the presence of another dragon!" added Nehebkau.

Pyrra saw Ying for the first time and Angus noticed that the lad stood frozen to the spot with his mouth wide open.

"Who's this?" asked Pyrra cautiously.

Angus explained all about Yingjie and his grandfather's kidnapping. As the Chinese lad became less shocked he added to his story and Pyrra eventually began to relax a little more. She was still worried about Wymarc though and looked to the skies for his return. After another ten minutes of waiting Angus decided that he has had enough and wanted to go in. The Chinese lad immediately agreed and even Pyrra said nothing to persuade Angus from his course.

The two dragons landed in the middle of a cobbled courtyard after flying over the outer wall and both Ying and Angus jumped from Pyrra's back. Angus scanned the surroundings for any sign of Wymarc but nothing stirred except the bare wintery branches some trees off to the left. At one end of the courtyard there was a long stair case with a twisting dragon depicted down the centre of the stone. On either side of the courtyard were a series of smaller buildings in various shapes and sizes. The roofs were ornately tiered and decorated with many carvings on the corner of every tier. The carvings appeared to be of strange looking beasts that Angus could barely make out.

"There's always a procession of mythical beasts guarding the Imperial palaces and depending how important the building dictated how many animals guarded it!" explained Ying in reply to Angus' curious look. "See, the back marker is always a dragon."

"That's a good place for a dragon to hide!" replied Angus.

"Really... My grandfather had one on his house but when I returned it was lying on the ground smashed to pieces!" added Ying.

The low roofed building at the top of the stairs appeared empty and they decided it was best to split up and check the buildings out more thoroughly. Angus and Pyrra went off towards the right and Kadin went left with Nehebkau leaving Ying to climb the dragon stairway right up to the front entrance.

Chapter 29

'Nemesis'

Angus looked inside yet another empty room and by the looks of it the place had been empty for some time. They had been searching for only 15 minutes but the young protector was bored by lack of action and he kicked a small pebble along the ground in frustration. The pebble hit something and he looked up to see Wymarc standing a few yards away.

"Sorry Wymarc I didn't see you there!" said Angus. Pyrra joined him from the other side of the building.

"I have found Georgina and she needs your help... follow me" said Wymarc and without waiting he turned and began to walk off.

"Wait!" shouted Angus, "What's wrong with her?"

"Please Angus you must come quickly" replied Wymarc before setting off again.

Both Pyrra and the boy exchanged worried glances and Angus was suspicious of the dragon's strange behaviour. But nevertheless they followed him as they were desperate to find Georgina and welcomed the news that she really was nearby.

Wymarc led Angus and Pyrra into the main building, through large doors and into a large symmetrical throne room. Angus' subconscious screamed at him as he realised it was the place from his dreams. What was different was that it appeared to be empty of the many people he had seen in the frequent visitations he had made with the mysterious blue dragon. As in his dreams the floor was paved with stone and it was devoid of furniture except for an embroidered screen at one end and a large peacock throne in front of it. Both sat on a large podium and that's when he saw what was trussed up in the foreground. On the floor he saw Ying and Kadin lying back to back on the bare floor with their hands and feet bound. Both boys struggled and fought against their bonds and when they saw Angus they fought all the more frantically.

"Angus, get Pyrra away before it's too late!" shouted Kadin.

Nehebkau appeared from a large side door and Angus was confused as the green dragon just walked up to the boys and stood idly beside them. He did not seem to be concerned about their plight and it became even more bizarre when Wymarc walked up to the other side of the boys and did the same.

"What are you two playing at? Help them!" shouted Pyrra, equally frustrated by her friends' actions.
Angus could not understand why the dragons were not helping the boys and was even more stunned when Meredith walked out from behind the richly embroidered screen and promptly sat in the peacock throne with a triumphant look on her face, drumming her long fingernails on the carved armrest.

Both Pyrra and Angus stood dumbfounded by what they saw and Pyrra pleaded with the other dragons again, but they did not respond. Angus noticed that their eyes had a faraway look in them and he knew something extremely serious was wrong.

"Good morning Angus!" crooned Meredith, "Are you not going to greet an old friend?"

"Nehebkau... do something... don't just stand there!" shouted Angus.

"It's no use they work for me now and will only do as I command!" said Meredith grinning from the throne.

"Release my friends and show where you have Georgina and I won't tell the police about this" bargained Angus.

Meredith just laughed as the two boys continued to plead with Angus to send Pyrra away from the scene.

"She has put a spell on them and they don't know us anymore!" shouted Kadin.

Angus ignored them and advanced on Meredith.

"Wait! Don't you want to see your little girlfriend again?" purred the heiress. "Bring her out!"

Georgina was pushed out from behind the screen and she too had her hands tied, and was also gagged. Angus began to walk towards her and as he did so he saw she had fear in her eyes and looked anxiously to her left. When he looked more closely at his distraught friend he could see a dragon's claw on her shoulder and that she was restrained. She walked further away from the screen and the dark and foreboding body of a dragon appeared from behind the partition.

His mind reeled as he realised all his worst nightmares had come true; Felspar was alive!

"Get behind me Angus!" growled Pyrra.

Reluctantly the lad obeyed but he could see the tears running down Georgina's cheeks as her body shook with fear. The boys on the floor stayed silent as they watched apprehensively, wondering what was going to happen.

"Pleased to see me?" he snarled.

"Not particularly" growled Pyrra.

"I'm going to finish what I started and then I'm going to eat that little pipsqueak beside you!" spat Felspar fiercely. Angus looked up at Pyrra, but she was too focused on her opponent to acknowledge him.

"Perhaps I will finish what Angus started... how is your chest... does it hurt much?" replied Pyrra.
Felspar unfurled his wings and snarled menacingly at his adversary, clearly infuriated at the mention of the injury he sustained in their last meeting. The large black dragon started to circle around to get clear of the podium and have clear floor space between him and his target. Angus could see the muscles in Pyrra's body grow taut as she prepared to pounce and an equally ready Felspar steadied himself for attack. The other two dragons just stood and watched as Angus, helpless, knew he could not help his friends. Both dragons crouched like cats, ready to pounce on their prey and then suddenly Meredith stood up.

"I command you to stop!"
To Angus' complete astonishment his friend did exactly that.

"Felspar please come here, and do stop teasing our guests. Pyrra, please sit down"

Like a trained dog the green dragon sat down quietly, folding her wings around her, just as the other dragons were seated!

Chapter 30

'All in Vain'

Felspar grinned maliciously as he sauntered over to
Meredith while Angus ran to Pyrra and pleaded with her to
speak to him.

"Pyrra... what are you doing?" he shouted, "This isn't
funny!"

The green dragon ignored him completely as the young
protector desperately tried to get her attention. The dragon
just stared at him blankly as if he were a stranger. The
whole thing was a nightmare, but unlike the ones he had
recently, this was one he could not wake up from! Both
Meredith and Felspar laughed at the boy's frustration. 'Was
this what the blue dragon wanted to show him? That he
was going to lose his best friend to some magic trick
conjured up by a mad woman!' Meredith held out her hand
and beckoned him.

"Angus come here... it's no use trying to speak to her
as the dragons will only obey me now" she explained.

"What have you done to them?" shouted Angus angrily.

"You should be more worried about what I'm going to
do to you!" spat Meredith nastily. "It was so good of you to
save me the trouble of coming to find you in the UK and I

might have missed you had it not been for my efficient receptionist passing on a message that two young boys were looking for me in my Hong Kong office. I'm flattered that you came all this way to see me!"

"Don't be!" snarled Angus. "I only want my friend back and you had better not have harmed her!" continued the lad as he glanced at Georgina who looked very frightened.

"I don't think you're in any position to make threats Angus" replied Meredith laughing. "Take them to the cells!" she shouted at the dragons.

The dragons duly obeyed Meredith's orders and proceeded to take the teenagers to the cells. Angus struggled and protested as he and the others were taken away. Pyrra picked him up by the clothing with her teeth and unceremoniously carried him out of the throne room. Wymarc carried the two boys as Nehebkau led Georgina into the courtyard and across the cobbled stones to a smaller building on the far side of the palace. As they reached the smaller buildings they were met by two men and led further back to a dirty looking structure tucked behind the more ornately decorated palace structures. The guards took over and led the four teens into the dingy building. Angus recognised the two guards as the men he met on the rooftop of Meredith's offices in London. They nearly caught him that time, but somehow he managed to make himself invisible to them and he wished he could do it again now!

"Well, look who we have here Ron!" said one of the guards.

"This is the little blighter that caused us all the trouble last year!" replied the larger man.

The big man grabbed Angus roughly and tried to force the boy into a cell, but Angus resisted by grabbing the door frame.

"Get in there before I give you a hiding!" said the man as he picked Angus up and tossed him inside.

Angus picked himself up from the floor and ran to the door in frustration, but he merely bounced off the solid wood. Anger boiled inside him and he kicked the door and beat it, shouting his frustration at his captors. He turned and paced inside the cell like a caged animal, his fury filling his thoughts. After a while he began to study the thick walls and the solid door of his cell, and realised that things were hopeless. Dejectedly Angus walked to the wall and kicked it hard. It did not help his situation in any way as the stone was thick and solid, but it was the last act of defiance and although it hurt his foot he felt better for it. He turned his back against the wall and slumped down to the floor, sliding his back down the wall to sit down heavily. The young protector sat with his head in his hands for some time. The events of the last few days played through his mind again and again. Each time he did this he got more and more depressed at how easy it had been for Meredith to catch them. He was exhausted from the amount of travelling they had done and from the stress of the situation he now found himself in. Even Pyrra had turned against him! Eventually he lay down and succumbed to sleep.

Someone was calling to him and for a change it was not the blue dragon. He guessed it would not be back to pester him since he was already where he was supposed to be, but the person calling him was persistent. He realised it was Georgina's voice and he started to wake up. Angus found himself lying on a cold stone floor with no one in his cell but him. His back hurt from sleeping in the most uncomfortable position he had ever been in and he thought he must have dreamt Georgina's voice since she was in another cell.

"Angus; are you okay?" said the disembodied voice of Georgina, "Why won't you answer me?"

The young lad looked about him confused until he realised that her voice was coming from a grating in the stone floor. Angus immediately stooped towards it and answered.

"Yeah, I'm fine... I was just sleeping" he replied.

"Sleeping!" she replied, "How can you sleep at a time like this?"

"Well it's been a bit of a journey and I've not been getting much sleep!" he replied sheepishly.

"Angus" called Kadin suddenly, "I'm here with Ying in the cell next to yours I think!"

"Hey guys... Georgina, are you alright?" asked Angus.

"Yes I am no thanks to that nasty woman..." replied the girl, emotions cracking her voice, "If you only knew what she put me through!"

"I'm sorry I didn't get here sooner..." said Angus but his voice fell away as it all seemed a bit pointless now that they were all captured and locked up.

"I low on earth did you find me?" asked Georgina. Their voices were faint but audible and now that they all realised they could use the floor drains that linked the rooms like a kind of speaking tube, they could at least communicate.

"Well that's a long story and one I'll keep for now... Why did she bring you here and what has she done to Pyrra and the others?"

"She made me crawl into a tunnel system somewhere north of here and I had to get an object for her... I didn't know what it was for, and she told me they had captured you and would hurt you if I didn't cooperate!" explained Georgina, "It would have been better... if I'd never come out of there!" she added as she started to breakdown.

"I'm sorry Georgina, I should have been with you!" replied Angus quietly.

Suddenly a strange voice sounded quietly through the drain.

"Nothing you could have done would have avoided this outcome" said an old man.

"Grandfather!" shouted Ying, immediately drawing hushes from the others.

"Yes Ying I am here... Are you okay?" replied the lad's grandfather.

"I'm fine, but what happened to you?" answered Ying. "Why didn't you tell me dragons were real?"

Ying was happy to hear that his grandfather was alive and unharmed, but obviously rather annoyed the old man had kept such a secret from him.

"I tried to, but you were too focused on the future; turning your back on the old ways, remember!" answered the old man sagely.

Through this drain system they discovered that the old man was held captive in another cell and had been there for several weeks. He had also been talking to Georgina since she was brought to the cells on Saturday evening and he had explained a few things to the poor girl.

The old man began to tell the story of how he had been captured by Felspar and forced to divulge the secret location of the object Meredith had been searching for.

"But if it's been a secret for a thousand years how did she know about it?" asked Angus.

"The SSDP records!" answered Georgina. "Remember when she was caught stealing some of the information from Calmor. This was surely one of the things she uncovered!"

"You mean she is now able to control all dragons?" asked Kadin.

"I'm afraid so" replied You Longwei. "Meredith is able to control any dragon with the Silver Claw and that is why she must be stopped before she gains access to the Realm Beyond."

The old man was sure that no one would know what he was talking about, but he was about to be proved mistaken.

"So the hidden realm of the Asian dragons is real?" asked Angus.

"Yes and I am surprised you know about this; but Felspar is already trying to track down the clues to its location" replied the old man. "If they find it, Meredith will have an army of dragons at her disposal!"

You Longwei went on to explain about his family's role over the last thousand years and how they had kept the location of the Silver Claw secret for so long.

"I have shamed my forefathers with my failure" he finished after giving them an account of his capture.

"You can morph?" asked Angus incredulously.

"Yes I can... but it took me 80 years to learn how to do it!"

Angus was impressed and it made him wonder if he really had developed some powers. After all, he had managed to avoid detection last year on the roof and then there was the incident with the bullies. He really did need to have that chat with Godroi!

As the day wore on Georgina brought them up to speed about her adventures and how she came close to death. The old man explained that she was protected by her silver brooch, and only because it was made of the same precious metal as the claw. Meredith and Felspar would not have known this and had surely sent the girl to her death when they forced her down there.

"It was providence that you were chosen young lady and had you not had that combination you would not have been able to get the claw" added You Longwei. "The Wyrm was also controlled by the Silver Claw which is why it went away when you told it to."

"Yes, but where's all this got us now!" wailed Georgina. "I've given Meredith the ultimate power over all dragons and that was exactly what she wanted…"

"This is not your fault" said the old man. "It was destiny and there is nothing you could have done to change it!" The group knew he was right and reassured Georgina that she should not blame herself. Ying and his grandfather You Longwei began to talk to each other privately for a few minutes, catching up on things. Angus listened with interest as it was obvious to him that the old man could possibly help him understand some of the things that had happened to him since meeting Pyrra. You Longwei asked about the Secret Society of Dragon Protectors and as Angus and the rest of them settled down for the night,

Kadin explained how things had developed over the past 2 years. The bolt of a door slid open and Angus warned them to be careful in case the guards heard them. The group quietened down as the guards entered the hallway outside the cells and checked the prisoners one by one. Angus pretended to be asleep and the men soon went back to whatever room they occupied. The young protector felt reassured by the fact that they were all unharmed and held in the same building, but wondered what Meredith had in store for them now she had possession of the Silver Claw. He hoped she would just let them go; however he knew it was not safe to presume anything with that woman. Angus finally drifted off to sleep on the floor of his cell and no sooner had his eyes closed when he was visited in his sleep by the blue dragon again.

"I thought I'd seen the last of you!" he said. "Well I'm here and a fat lot of good you were!"

"Use your powers to escape Draca Gast; use your powers!"

Chapter 31

'A Neat Trick'

Angus awoke, sat bolt upright and started fumbling for the bedside lamp switch next to his bed before he remembered where he was. He rubbed the sleep from his eyes and stared around at his gloomy cell. It had bare stone walls, high ceilings, no window and an extremely solid wood door, which was the only way in or out. The drainage grating in the floor was barely big enough for a cat to get through and the door had a very small opening with two very solid bars lodged solidly inside the wood.

"How am I supposed to escape from here!" he said to himself.

The young protector could not work out what he was supposed to do or what powers he was supposed to use. He knew he could somehow tap into Pyrra's mind when they were both concentrating, and although he was getting very good at it, he did not know if she would be able to respond in her current hypnotic state. He could not really see how this could help him escape from their current predicament; especially with Felspar out there and Meredith controlling everything. He heard Georgina calling him softly through the drain, trying not to disturb the others.

Angus was amazed that anyone was managing to sleep at all as it was very uncomfortable on the cold stone floor and it really was bitterly cold.

"Hi Georgina... how are you?" he whispered in reply.

"I'm fine now that you're here" she answered.

"Fat lot of good I've done!" he said.

"You came all this way looking for me... that means more than you know" she replied softly.

Angus was glad she could not see him as he had blushed at her last comment. He wanted to tell her how much he liked her but did not think this was the right moment.

"You were really brave in those tunnels you know" he said, changing the subject.

"I was petrified the whole time and was lucky not to be eaten by that Wyrm... you would have coped better!" she replied.

"No way!" he whispered. "You were awesome... I would have still been stuck in the first tunnel!"

As she lay on her back in her cell the girl smiled at the praise, then she remembered something she had meant to ask the night before.

"I asked you before how you found me and you avoided the question... A few things have happened

recently and you won't let me in... What's going on
Angus?" she probed.

The young lad was caught in two minds about telling her of
the things that had happened to him, and decided that if he
could not trust Georgina, then who could he trust? The
truth had to come out soon enough and he began to
explain about the blue dream dragon and all the strange
things that had happened to him over the past year or so.

When Angus had finished the brief account and that he
had been sort of guided to her, he paused for some sort of
reaction.

"What do you think?"

"I don't know Angus... It's hard to say exactly what this
blue dragon is or what it is trying to get you to do" she
replied after some thought.

Unbeknown to the whispering pair, the old man,
You Longwei had listened in on every word. He smiled and
nodded as he shifted position on the floor, lying close to
the grate to hear better; and trying hard to make his old
bones more comfortable.

The rattle of keys and clanging of pots heralded the
dawn of day, and Angus truly wished with all his heart that
he was not there. The guards made their way round the
prisoners, delivering warm Chinese tea and bowls of rice

one by one. Kadin and Ying were first to get some food. Then Georgina took her rations gratefully and began to eat the rice with her fingers. The old man thanked the guards and carefully placed his food on the floor beside him as he knew he would not have time to eat it anyway.

"Obviously not hungry that one" said Ron the larger guard.

"Probably going on hunger strike!" replied Jeff.
Both men laughed as they locked the old man's cell and moved to Angus'. When they unlocked the door of the young dragon protector's cell, the boy was nowhere to be seen.

"This is not good Ron!" said Jeff, his face chalk white.

"She's gonna feed us to them bleedin' dragon's Jeff" replied Ron.
Angus could not work out what they were going on about as he was sitting on the floor facing them. He was about to say something when he realised he had somehow wished himself invisible again. He closed his eyes and concentrated on being invisible with all the concentration he could muster.
Both the guards were fraught as they knew they would be for it when the boss found out that her prime captive had escaped from under their very noses. The guards threw

down the boy's breakfast and ran out like headless chickens.

Angus could not believe his luck! As the guards scurried off to search further afield, Angus quickly picked himself up from the floor and looked out from his open cell door. In their panic the guards had left his cell open and not only that, they had left the keys in the lock as well. Angus wasted no further time and grabbed the keys. He released the other four prisoners as quickly as he could. Georgina dove into his arms when she saw him and he gave her a reassuring hug. Now they had to set about finding a way out of the palace, but not without the dragons.

"How did you get out?" asked Kadin looking puzzled.

"It's a bit hard to explain... perhaps we should think of a plan to get out of here... The guards won't stay outside much longer!" replied Angus successfully evading the awkward question; although he noticed that the old man smiled at him knowingly.

Based on their early morning conversation, Georgina had already guessed how he had escaped the guards; however the other two were completely puzzled by the whole thing, but just happy to be out of the cells in any case.

"So what's the plan?" asked Ying.

Angus knew that they had no choice, but to first get out from the jail building and then get the Silver Claw from Meredith. It would be the only way to break her hold over their dragons and free them. Angus quickly explained what he thought they should do and having received full backing; the entourage filed outside. Ying checked to see if the coast was clear and having found no sign of the guards they quickly ran to some trees behind the main palace. It turned out that the trees were part of an ornate garden and they were able to use the shrubbery as cover to hide in. As Angus suspected the men soon came back with Meredith and she screamed orders at them to go and search for the escaped prisoners.

"Find them for me Felspar... I want them back in those cells!" she said turning to the black dragon.

The escapees felt vulnerable outside and decided to head for the palace and find a way inside as quickly as possible.

The main building was surprisingly easy to enter and whatever security had been there was surely outside searching for them. They split up to search more effectively with Angus and Georgina making up one team and the other two lads and You Longwei making up the other. Most of the palace comprised of corridors with sliding partitions; each screen hiding another room or corridor. It was like a giant puzzle and Angus and Georgina carefully made their way through the rooms looking for Meredith's chamber. Eventually they found a room with simple furniture in it and a bed which they assumed to be Meredith's lodgings. Angus could not believe his luck when he saw the Silver Claw lying on a big wooden chest.

"Wait here and watch" he whispered as he motioned to Georgina.

The girl stayed behind him to stand guard as he tiptoed in through the open door. The wooden floor boards creaked as he slowly crept towards the Silver Claw. The light shone off the silver metal and glinted enticingly as he reached his hand forward to pick it up. As he went to grasp the claw he felt elated and almost free of gravity and that's when he realised he was floating off the floor. He tried desperately to grab the claw as he was lifted several feet into the air!

Chapter 32

'Live Nightmare'

Angus almost had the claw within his grasp, but instead he now dangled in the air, held up by his jacket. He struggled and arched his neck back in an attempt to see who his captor was when a familiar female voice barked.

"Not so fast young man!"

He turned in the direction of the voice to see Meredith standing in the doorway, eyes blazing. She had one of Georgina's arms firmly lodged behind her back. The young girl struggled as well but could not speak as Meredith had her free hand over the girl's mouth. The heiress grinned as she twisted Georgina's wrist a little more behind her back causing the young protector to wince in pain and submit.

"Leave her alone!" roared Angus, thrashing his legs and striking up at whatever held him.

He managed to spin around and found himself staring into the blazing red eyes of Felspar as he dangled the lad in his jaws. The black dragon looked enraged and a low and menacing growl emanated from between clenched teeth. Felspar's lip curled up to reveal razor sharp teeth that would easily rip Angus apart should he decide to and the lad went limp as he realised the uselessness of struggling any further.

A few minutes later Angus found himself dropped from a great height onto the floor of the throne room and just in front of where Pyrra sat on her haunches like a house cat. The young protectors now found themselves guarded by their own dragons; Angus was in the centre of the room and the others off to one side. Behind him Meredith questioned her guards as to how the prisoners in their care managed to escape.

"We can't explain it Ma'am... he just weren't there when we opened the cell... it was like he vanished into thin air!" explained Jeff, the smaller of the two men.
Her sardonic laughter could be heard all around the empty chamber.

"Indeed... Then we will just need to speak to the troublemaker and ask him how he did it!" she snapped. Angus felt the chill run up his spine as he realised where he was and that he knew exactly what was about to happen next. His pulse raced as he turned around slowly. Just as he feared he was now in a room full of the same people and dragons he had seen in his dreams many times. He was in the same large but simply decorated room and in it stood the same guards he could now recognise. It was his nightmare coming to life and he struggled to comprehend it all. He looked to the left and sure enough Georgina and Kadin stood beside Ying and then his grandfather You Longwei. The old man looked at Angus and winked his knowing smile now as familiar to the boy as anything else he took for granted. The dragons were there sitting like trained animals waiting for an order; and all with the same glazed look on their faces.

"Tell me Angus, how did you manage to escape my guards?" asked Meredith.

Shocked by the fact that his dream was coming true, Angus could not answer. 'What had the blue dragon from his dreams been trying to show him?' he thought wildly. 'Surely it was supposed to mean something; how was it going to help him!'

"No witty remarks? Perhaps he needs a little persuasion!" growled a voice from behind him.

Angus spun as he recalled who had said this and not more than two metres away from him was Felspar; right on cue!

"Now, now Felspar; you leave him be" purred Meredith, "I have a much better method of dealing with this little thorn!"

Felspar sneered as he walked past Angus to join Meredith; the young protector watched in stunned silence as the black dragon swaggered to Meredith's side. Angus knew what was coming next and this was the start of the worst passage of his nightmare.

"Pyrra, I command you to kill Angus Munro!" shouted Meredith maniacally.

In the same painfully slow way Angus turned to face Pyrra. In his dream he had never been able to understand why this was happening but now he knew the why. The question was what good was it going to do him? He knew what was coming and as he looked up into Pyrra's green eyes he could once again see a glimmer of who she really was and the conflict within her. The green dragon's body vibrated as she fought to resist the order.

"Attack him now, Pyrra!" screamed Meredith. "I command you to kill him!"

This was it and sure enough Pyrra's eyes glazed over with a faraway look. A stranger now gazed upon him and as her body stopped vibrating Pyrra reared in front of him and, with her right claw raised high, prepared to attack him!

"Now this little spectacle I am going to enjoy" Meredith sneered to Felspar.

"Pyrra it's me, Angus, remember?" he shouted. "Pyrra, please, it's me!"

Bizarrely he had the strangest of thoughts 'Hold on; Meredith never said that in the dream before!' But this was drowned out as Meredith's laughter got louder and louder and Pyrra prepared to slash downwards with her claw.

"Angus!" screamed Georgina as she started to cry. 'Again another new thing; perhaps that meant something' he thought anxiously and her best friends dragon eyes narrowed on him. He knew that this was the point he had never managed to get past. The part of the nightmare he had never been able to deal with.

Without warning Pyrra's fore claw slashed downwards; her defenceless prey rooted to the spot. Her claws connected with the floor directly below where Angus stood. Meredith stood open mouthed at what she had just witnessed. The old man smiled broadly, nodding his head as he witnessed Angus' display of power. The young protector had somehow dodged the attack.

"What are you playing at Pyrra? Kill him now!" screeched Meredith angrily.

Angus lay several feet from the blow that would surely have sliced him in two. He had somehow managed to dive to one side, but to dodge her that fast meant he was somehow using Dragon Time. He had done this once before in similar circumstances and he hoped he would still be able to do it as Pyrra rounded on him for another strike.

"Please Pyrra... stop this and come back to me!" he called out to her.

The green dragon sprang forward suddenly and snapped her jaws in his direction only to miss him again. This time Angus had stayed on his feet and he continued trying to break the spell she was under. He was now in new territory as this had never happened in his dreams. They never got that far, but the reality had also been slightly different from the previous versions he had dreamt. Surely this meant that dreams were not always cast in stone. He glanced at the black dragon and remembered that Felspar had tried to go back in time to change it and thus alter the future. It occurred to Angus that the future could perhaps be influenced. Maybe he was not supposed to die after all and he would somehow get through to Pyrra. He quickly tumbled to one side as another strike swung down from above. Twice more he dodged Pyrra's snapping jaws as he continued to probe her for some reaction.

"Come on Pyrra... come back to me... please" he pleaded.

The green dragon swiped at Angus again and as he side stepped neatly to escape her only to be immediately caught by her tail as it whipped around to counter his manoeuvre. The blow caught him square in the chest and knocked him into a wall. He lay winded on the floor and could only watch in horror as his beloved dragon towered over him.

"Pyrra... please..." he managed to say as he winced in pain.

The green dragon paused and shook her head groggily like someone trying to awaken from a deep sleep. This delay did not sit well with Meredith and she grew impatient with Pyrra's lack of urgency.

"What are you waiting for... finish him!" she bellowed. Angus looked up at his best friend and could see the torment within her eyes. She stared back at him almost pleadingly as she fought inwardly against the commands she had been given. Angus could feel her mind starting to reach out to him and he closed his eyes to concentrate on her; calling out to her subconscious with all his will. Meredith strode over to Pyrra and shouted at her again, repeating the order from her diminutive height.

"I order you to kill him!" she growled nastily as she held the Silver Claw upwards. "Do it now!"

Angus opened his eyes when he heard this, his concentration broken and he stared malevolently into the eyes of Meredith. The woman grinned madly as Pyrra raised her claw higher and disbelievingly Angus stared up into the eyes of Pyrra.

"No!" screamed Georgina as the green claw swung downwards.

Chapter 33

'Morgant'

Not wanting to witness the demise of her friend,
Georgina buried her face in her hands as Pyrra struck. But
the dragon had not aimed at Angus! Instead the dragon's
blow swung at Meredith and knocked the Silver Claw from
the mad woman's hand. The spell on the other dragons
was instantly broken and they shook their heads as the fog
that had enveloped their minds lifted. Felspar stepped
forward bristling with anger and ready for a fight, but the
other dragons had recovered their wits enough to confront
him. They rounded on Felspar as he tried to get to Angus
and a vicious battle started between the dragons as they
exacted revenge for being hypnotised and controlled.
Wymarc and Felspar reared up and Angus watched as
they snapped ferociously at each other. Nehebkau charged
the guards with a fierce growl and Kadin, Georgina, Ying
took advantage of this as the turned on their jailors to fight
them fiercely. Georgina caught one man with a right hook
that hurt her hand and Ying temporarily crippled his captor
with a sharp kick to the inside of the man's knee. They
both turned to help You Longwei, but stood stunned as
they watched the old man nimbly take out two men with a

series of martial art moves that defied his years and left the guards nursing several bruises as they escaped the onslaught. The three then took refuge on the far side of the throne room away from the brawling dragons. Pyrra had sent Meredith sprawling but had not harmed the woman in any way. Unfortunately she was still intent in regaining control and Angus saw her scramble towards the Silver Claw. The young protector instantly sprung forward and grabbed the Silver Claw just before her fingernails reached it.

"Stop!" shouted Angus, his voice echoing around the large room.

Instantly all the dragons stopped fighting and turned to face Angus. Even Pyrra was subdued by his command and the boy could feel the power he wielded. He looked into Pyrra's eyes and saw the same glazed look she had earlier.

"Pyrra, I give you your freedom from this" he said to her.

The dragon instantly became herself again and he ran to her and hugged her before he also released Wymarc and Nehebkau from the spell.

"Felspar, I command you to pick up Meredith and hold her there until I tell you otherwise!" he said.

The black dragon walked forward almost robotically and grabbed hold of Meredith, pinning her to the floor; while the woman screamed in irate frustration.

"We should probably round up the guards and put them in the cells" added Pyrra.

"That's a good idea... let's go get them" replied Wymarc.

"Do you think it's safe to leave these two here?" asked Nehebkau.

"Just remind Felspar of his duty Angus" said Pyrra. The protector repeated his command as Meredith screamed in frustration. The black dragons red eyes reflected the faraway look of a dragon under the spell of the Silver Claw.

The escapees quickly got things in order by capturing the men Meredith had brought to China and locked them all in a cell, but Angus had some questions for Pyrra.

"How did you manage to break the spell?" he asked.

"Our bond Angus..." she replied. "It was too great and in the end the spell could not break it!"

"I'm glad it did as I thought I had lost you!" he replied.

"Somehow though I think you knew I was going to attack you!" she asked pointedly.

Angus looked up at her green eyes and realised he had not done a good job in keeping his nightmares a secret, but then it was difficult when you had a mental bond such as theirs.

"I've been having these dreams about a blue dragon and when he visited he kept showing me this place and that you would be forced to attack me!" he replied honestly, deciding to tell her the truth.

"Indeed..." she replied, but seeing the others coming back to join them she added, "This is very interesting and you will need to tell me more when we are able to speak in private."

Her protector nodded his agreement and they joined the others.

None of the dragons had met You Longwei and he was introduced to them and the old man told them the story of his family ancestry. They had played an important part of protecting the Silver Claw and the Realm Beyond where the Asian dragons had gone to live. Throughout his conversation the old man referred to the dragons that had chosen to depart the earth and leave mankind to its own destruction.

"They are content to live there and they have found a haven where they can live in peace. That peace has not come cheaply and many thousands of years ago they fought a great battle against the strongest of dragons, a Wyvern called Morgant"

"I thought he was just a myth!" said Pyrra interrupting.

"There are a lot of dragons who wish he was, but he is quite real and was the owner of that claw before it was ripped from his flesh" answered the old man.

"You mean this Morgant had silver claws?" asked Angus fascinated.

"He did and what's more he could control other dragons" replied You Longwei.

"Then how was he defeated?" asked Kadin.

"Well, some say his ego got the better of him, but others tell of Draca Gast!" explained the old man.
Pyrra glanced at Angus when You Longwei said this and Angus knew she was recalling the first time she heard that name. It was when they first met Barfoot in the birthing caves of Krubera and she had found it strange that the venerable dragon had used it to refer to Angus. The old man just stood grinning at Angus knowingly, and the lad wondered just how much more he could tell him about Draca Gast; the Dragon Spirit.

"I see from your face that you are familiar with this name... do you know the meaning?" asked You Longwei.

"Yes we do... but what is the connection between this Draca Gast of ancient times and Angus?" asked Pyrra.

"Long ago Draca Gast was one of the original protectors; before the SSDP. A group of men dedicated to preserving the realm of the dragons and their kind..." explained You Longwei, who now had the attention of the whole group. "Not only did they protect the realm from mankind but they also intervened in a war between dragons."

"Dragons fought against each other?" asked Kadin, shocked.

"Not really the dragons as such, but dragon kind" he replied. "You see Wyverns were not really counted as dragons. They are far larger than dragons and walk on two legs... a bit like a Tyrannosaurus-Rex with wings."
The protectors tried to imagine what that would look like and all of them pictured a menacing and fierce creature in their minds,

"The Wyverns were not as adaptable as the dragons and they died out over the years, but one remained and it was only his powers that made him virtually invulnerable" continued the old man.

"Are you trying to tell me that Morgant could still be alive?" asked Pyrra seriously.

"He can't be Pyrra..." countered Wymarc, "that would make him..."

"The oldest living creature!" stated You Longwei as he finished what Wymarc was about to say.
The dragons were stunned by this revelation.

"But surely he was just a tale ours mothers used to tell us to frighten us when we were bad... You know... You had better behave or Morgant will get you!" added Wymarc.

"I really wish that were true but based on the information passed down through my family, he was very real and could still be alive!" answered You Longwei.

"What do you mean, wasn't he killed?" asked Georgina.

"No he wasn't as he was a very difficult dragon to overcome. It would need a tremendous amount of power to end his life and no one was able to do that. He could control other dragons due to some magic he had developed. This was manifested in one particular silver claw and it was Draca Gast that eventually duped him by literally clipping his toes" explained the old man as he chuckled at his own joke.

"How did Draca Gast win?" asked Angus.

"Not much is remembered about that but it is said that Draca Gast lured the Wyvern into a trap that took his claw and he was somehow trapped in a dungeon realm that could only be accessed through the Realm Beyond" answered You Longwei.

"So what your saying is that this Morgant is trapped in a dungeon realm and could come back to attack us all?" asked Wymarc.

"Meredith knows where the first clue to the hidden realm is and if she finds it she could be foolish enough to try and use Morgant to get what she wants" added the old man. "She will need to be stopped before she can get everyone into more trouble. I don't think she knows about Morgant but she does know about the Realm Beyond and I don't see her as the type to give up easily!"

"Don't worry about her... the only place she is going is back to the UK to have her arrested again for kidnapping Georgina!" replied Angus.

Suddenly a thought struck him and he turned and started to run back to the palace. They ran into the throne room and Angus immediately saw what he had hoped he would not; it was empty!

Chapter 34

'Warning'

Felspar had somehow broken the spell of the Silver Claw and escaped. By the looks of it he had obviously taken Meredith with him and the young protector kicked the doorway in frustrated anger.

"I should have known he would break the spell!" he shouted.

"But how could you?" asked Georgina in a sympathetic tone.

"Because I could see that he was fighting the commands I gave him... I saw the same in Pyrra when she was attacking me... Why didn't I make sure... so stupid!" he replied before kicking the doorway again.

Georgina put a hand on his shoulder to calm him down and it worked instantly. She gave him a hug and she felt relieved when he relaxed and hugged her back.

"Thank you for coming for me" she whispered into his ear.

As always, he blushed bright red with embarrassment and immediately tried to act more manly when he saw the other lads grinning at him.

"I think we should probably search the place... just in case they are still here..." he said gruffly.

The others nodded and went off in search of the escapees, but they knew the duo would be long gone by now. Now Angus would definitely need to track down the hidden realm and warn the dragons within it about the danger Meredith posed. He wondered what they were like and if there were any humans there, but he guessed he would soon find out. Whoever they were they would need to wait as first he needed to get back to the UK and return Georgina to her father.

The preparations were made for the journey home and by this time Angus was so late he was not sure of how he would explain all of this to his mum and dad. Georgina had called her father to let him know she was safe and Angus had the unfortunate job of calling Calmor. Both Rathlin and Aurora ranted and raved down the phone line, taking it in turns to both commend him and criticise him, and he also got the blame for leading Kadin astray. Soon they had said goodbye to two new friends with the promise that they would return to visit and also to bring them to Calmor. Angus also wanted to know more about Draca Gast and what the connection was to him, but that would have to wait for another visit. Soon they were on their way home;

however this time they could take a more direct route which would hopefully trim some time off the journey. After only a few hundred miles Kadin and Nehebkau had to leave them as their route home was further south than the northerly route Angus and Georgina would take. They stopped on a remote hillside in China to say their goodbyes and the young girl gave Kadin a small hug.

"Thank you Kadin... I really appreciate that you went out of your way to save me" she said.

"You are most welcome Georgina and it was more down to his determination than mine that we managed to locate you" he replied honestly. "In shaa'Allah we will meet again soon under better circumstances!"

"I'm sure we will" she replied.

The two boys stood in front of each other and shook hands before Kadin put his free hand around Angus' shoulder and touched his right shoulder to the slightly surprised British lad. Angus hesitantly patted his friends back in return. Both protectors nodded at each other and smiled as they sat on the back of the dragon they protected. With a wave they were off on their separate ways.

Soon the ground below became a sheet of white making it difficult to make any features out at all. Angus looked over at Georgina and smiled as she slept while hugging Wymarc's neck; he decided to do the same. Before long his mind was full of the events of the last few days and he began to wonder if he would ever see the strange blue dragon ever again. He would like to thank him as he now realised the dragon had in fact been helping him all along. As soon as he thought it the dragon appeared in his mind.

"Greetings Angus!" said the dragon. "I am glad you are past this test and that you have saved your friend."

"You knew I was going to save her didn't you?" asked Angus.

"That is difficult to answer... I knew you were going to face this test of wills, but as to the result... let's just say that some things are never certain!"

This did not make much sense to Angus and he wondered what else might be in store for him.

"Can you tell me anything about the hidden realm?" he enquired.

"I'm afraid I cannot, but I can promise that whatever help I can provide you, it will be provided" replied the dragon.

"But how do I get in touch with you; where are you?" asked Angus in frustration.

"Nowhere you can visit physically Angus..." answered the blue dragon. "But I will be closer to you than you think and I will aid in whatever way possible; no matter the risk to myself!"

Now Angus was really confused, but the dream dragon went on;

"You now have possession of the Silver Claw and its power is too great for anyone to hold. It must be destroyed and no-one must be able to use it!" explained the dragon.

"But surely I can use it to help?" replied Angus.

"No!" replied the dragon, "It is too powerful and will eventually consume the user... the only way is to be rid of it forever... Do you understand?"

"Yes, I think I do" replied Angus quietly.

"A war is coming and it is one that you will play a key role in... you must be strong.... you must be strong... you must be..."

The dragon faded and Angus sat up and called out into the night sky.

"Wait for what?" asked Pyrra when she turned to look at him.

The steady and familiar beating of her wings sounded in his ears and it was somehow comforting to know that even the cruellest of spells woven, could not break their friendship and bond.

"It's nothing Pyrra" he smiled, "just a dream."

"Are you still getting visits then?"

"Yes, but it's okay... he's a friend and is only trying to help" replied Angus. "Where are we?"

"We're just north of the Black Sea... Krubera is to the south and behind us a bit" she replied pointing her nose in that direction. "I was tempted to visit but I think we should get back as quickly as we can!"

Angus agreed on that score, but he fished inside his jacket and brought out the Silver Claw. He turned it in his hands and now that he knew what it really was; it appeared more real to him than it did before.

"Pyrra do you think the Black Sea is very deep?" he asked.

"Yes I think it's reasonably so... why do you ask?"

"I just thought we could maybe take a slight detour over there... if that's okay with you."

When trying to come up with this story I wanted to touch Dubai in some way. Both Debi and I have lived here for so long that it only seemed fitting that we explored and extended the world of the SSDP in our own back yard. In truth it fits in well with the larger storyline of the books and hopefully we are guiding each book ever closer to the culmination of this larger theme. Only time and the stretch of my imagination will tell and I for one am looking forward to where this is going next... Anything is possible!

Debi Evans is overwhelmed by the success of The Secret Society of Dragon Protectors and enjoys going into schools to inspire children to read, and to write their own fantasy adventure stories. She loves travelling; using it as an excuse to check out the locations used in the books, so don't be surprised if the next book is set in South America or Africa! Writing with John is an absolute pleasure and she credits the longevity of their partnership to his infinite patience and singular vision. This book is especially for our United Arab Emirates based fans.

Look out for further books in the series.

THE SECRET SOCIETY
OF
DRAGON PROTECTORS

*For further details visit the official SSDP
website at*

www.thesecretsocietyofdragonprotectors.com